A Seductive Melody

The Kelly Brothers, Book 5
by
Crista McHugh

A Seductive Melody
Copyright 2014 by Crista McHugh
Edited by Gwen Hayes
Copyedited by Elizabeth MS Flynn
Cover Art by Sweet N' Spicy Designs

All rights reserved. This book or any portion thereof may not be reproduced or used in any manner whatsoever without the express written permission of the author or publisher except for the use of brief quotations in critical articles or reviews.

This is a work of fiction. Names, places, businesses, characters and incidents are either the product of the author's imagination or are used in a fictitious manner. Any resemblance to actual persons living or dead, actual events or locales is purely coincidental.

ISBN-13: 978-1-940559-88-9

A Seductive Melody

Chapter One

"*We admitted that we were powerless over our addiction, that our lives had become unmanageable.*"

No fucking shit.

Ethan Kelly read the rest of the *Twelve Steps of Narcotics Anonymous* and folded the single sheet of paper in half as the meeting was called to order. The two weeks' worth of stubble on his head felt foreign under his hand as he rubbed at it and glanced around the room. He'd shaved off his long black hair when he'd entered detox, a symbolic gesture of cutting off ties with his old life, but he still worried someone would recognize him and call him out. He wasn't there to put on a show for the media. He was there because he needed to stay clean, and this was one of the tools that had been recommended to him.

The inside of his left arm burned under his sleeve, and he rubbed the spot of his latest tattoo. Even though the flesh had healed, the pain behind it was still as raw as the day he'd gotten it.

The day he'd lost his best friend to heroin.

It was the wake-up call he'd both needed and been

dreading. He'd watched Tyler slip deeper and deeper into his addiction, but he'd been too scared to say something. Then it was too late to say anything. Two days after getting the tattoo, he checked himself into detox. He only wished he'd been able to do it with Ty. Instead, his best friend was now ashes in an urn, and Ethan was left trying to pick up the pieces of his shattered life alone.

The craving to say "fuck it all" and shoot up ambushed him. It would be so easy to get high and forget about the pain, to go back to the euphoric place where his muse reigned supreme and he didn't give a damn about anyone but himself and his music. He balled his hands into fists and squeezed his eyes shut. *I can do this. I have to do this. No more escaping reality.*

He drew in several deep cleansing breaths like they'd taught him to do during detox, and the craving subsided.

For now.

He opened his eyes just as a woman was sneaking into the chair across from him. She shrugged off her knee-length leather coat, giving him an ample view of the bare bit of her thigh between her cream-colored boots and mint green sixties-style mini-dress as she crossed her legs. A different craving rose within him, one that shot straight to his crotch. Thank god for the six feet of aisle space between them, or he'd be tempted to find out for himself if her skin was as silky and supple as it looked.

From the corner of her eye, she caught him staring. A flush rose up her neck and into her cheeks as she tugged on the hem of her skirt, but he couldn't turn away. Everything about her screamed Park Avenue, from her designer handbag to her flawless manicured nails. She looked like she should have been shopping at Neiman Marcus or Bergdorf Goodman, not sitting in a moldy church basement full of recovering addicts.

His attention wandered up from her legs to her face. He couldn't tell if her eyes were blue or green, but the arched brow above the left eye wordlessly asked him if he was done gawking.

And for the first time in two weeks, his lips rose into a grin. No, he wasn't done at all. Not as long as she had those legs on display.

She rolled her eyes and draped her coat over her lap, hiding those luscious thighs from his view just as the meeting leader, Gary, asked the new members to introduce themselves to the group.

Shit. This was the part he'd been dreading. Thankfully, he didn't have to give his last name, and he'd already been warned by Gary that he'd be hugged if he didn't make it clear from the beginning that he wasn't up for that. He cleared the lump forming in his throat and stood.

"Hi, I'm Ethan, and I'm not a hugger."

There. That was all they needed to know. The rest of his inner demons were his own to battle. He slumped back into his chair and crossed his arms, daring any of them to try and touch him.

"Hi, Ethan," the room replied in unison.

Then Gary opened the meeting up for the members to share.

Ethan stretched out his legs and closed his eyes, only halfway listening to their stories. He was here in this church basement only because his mother and the counselor at detox suggested he try it out. He didn't need any hand-holding or "Kumbaya" singing to help him avoid using again. He'd already gone through the flu-on-steroids hell of detox. And he had the most powerful deterrent to using again tattooed over his favorite vein.

Tyler Bransford, 1987–2014.

Every time he'd be tempted to shoot up, he'd see the name of his best friend and be reminded of the life and talent that were destroyed by heroin. To him, that was far more effective than a weekly meeting listening to people drone on and on about how hard it was to stay clean.

He had no idea how much time had passed, but when he cracked an eye open, he found the woman across the aisle studying him with a line furrowed above her too-perfect nose. Her lips were pursed as though he was some sort of riddle she was trying to decipher, yet despite the intense focus on her features, she twirled a lock of her dark brown hair around her fingers in a casual manner.

He mimicked the same questioning arched brow she'd given him.

Her lips parted in a silent gasp. She turned away and sat up straighter, her hands falling to her lap and her attention fixed on Gary instead of him.

Some part of him felt a little rush, knowing she'd been checking him out. The other part of him cautioned him to stay far away from Ms. Park Avenue. He already had enough drama going on in his life. He didn't need to involve what appeared to be a very high-maintenance woman. Not his style, anyway. He doubted she'd ever agree to hop on the back of his bike and zoom through the streets of Manhattan. He liked his women wild and fearless, not uptight and prissy.

Gary then announced it was time to adjourn and asked everyone to gather around in a circle for a quick prayer. Ethan's stomach recoiled at the idea. He didn't want any damned prayers or religion to be stuffed down his throat. And yet, he found himself joining the others and standing next to Ms. Park Avenue. She smelled of amber and sandalwood mingled with something soft and floral. Exotic, yet distinctly feminine. The intoxicating scent distracted him long enough to let his anger fizzle out, and by the time the prayer was finished, his gut was no longer in knots.

The circle disbanded, and Gary made his way to him. "I'll be with you in a minute, Ethan," he said before pulling Ms. Park Avenue aside. Their hushed conversation made Ethan wonder if he was reprimanding her for showing up late. A couple of minutes later, she nodded, and they both approached him.

"Ethan, I'd like you to meet Rebecca. Usually, we let our newcomers choose a sponsor after spending a few weeks getting to know the group, but I would like to personally recommend her as someone who can help you get settled into the program."

Why? Because I was checking her out?

"She has graciously agreed to help you until you choose a sponsor, if you're interested, and probably would understand your situation far better than most of us."

Ethan's mouth went dry. He'd already done so much to go underground while dealing with his addiction. Changed his appearance. Moved across the country from LA to New York. Avoided the media at all costs after dealing with the circus that had dogged him until he checked into detox. But he'd made the mistake of confiding his need for confidentiality to Gary, and now, the meeting leader had shared who he was with someone else. He ground his teeth and flexed his fingers. Maybe this had been a mistake after all.

Gary gave Rebecca a genuine smile and a nod, which she returned. "I'll let you two get better acquainted."

Ethan didn't dare move a muscle as the group leader left to talk to someone else, leaving him alone with her. Every nerve in his body stood on edge. If he wanted to keep his privacy, he couldn't reveal anything personal.

Her smile faltered into a nervous twitch of her lips. "Listen, Ethan, I know you may think this isn't for you, but please, give it another week or two. The first week is always the hardest. If you give it a chance—"

"What exactly did he say to you about me?"

"Well, he wasn't praising your sunny personality, that's for sure."

Her sarcasm caught him off guard, and despite his better judgment, he took a step toward her. "Then what did he say?"

"He said I of all people would know what you were going through, and he trusted that I would handle you with care until you feel ready to choose a sponsor."

His insides bristled at the thought of being handled with care. It was bad enough his mother was calling him every night to check on him like a child. "Did he say why?"

She shook her head, her dangling earrings rattling against her jaw. "Nope."

The whole situation perplexed him, and he took

another step toward her, encroaching on her personal space just to see how she'd react. "And who exactly are you?"

She looked up at him, and he finally could see the color of her eyes. Blue on the outside, green toward the center. Striking and clear and unwavering as she held his gaze. "A recovering addict, just like you."

His chest tightened, trapping the air in his lungs, but he refused to back down.

"In case you missed the memo," she continued, "the 'A' stands for 'anonymous.' It's something we take very seriously here. If you're still wondering why Gary thinks I'll be able to help you, I'd be willing to share a bit more about myself over coffee. But you'll have to wait until next week."

"Always a catch," he muttered before turning. But she intrigued him enough that he might come back just to find out who she was and what she was doing here.

"Think of it more as an enticement." She reached into her purse and pulled out a notepad and pen. "Here's my number. If you feel the need to shoot up, give me a call first, and I'll try to talk you down."

"Thanks for the vote of confidence." But he took the piece of paper with her number on it anyway. In any other situation, getting a sexy woman's digits meant he was doing something right. But right now, the fact she was giving him her number was a sign that she was just waiting for him to slip back into his old habits.

"Hey, I've been there, remember? I know what it's like to be new to this and how hard it is to say 'No' to the cravings. We all stumble. We all make mistakes. But we're not in this alone." She slipped her coat back on, her gaze raking him over from head to toe and back again. "And maybe next week, you'll have a better idea how I can help you out."

He could think of a dozen ways she could help him out, but none of them involved this support group. But he stepped aside to let her leave, watching the way her hips swayed as she walked. Yes, he definitely wanted to know Ms. Park Avenue's story.

He gathered up the booklets and pamphlets Gary had given him before the meeting and shoved them into his backpack. Rebecca's number, however, was carefully folded and slipped into the inner pocket of his wallet. He doubted he'd ever need it, but just in case…

His Ducati Streetfighter was parked half a block away. He strapped on his helmet and hopped on the bike, revving it up until the vibrating purr of the engine massaged away the tension in his muscles. He'd come back next week, if only to learn more about her. Then he kicked off and sped down the street before his doubts could catch up to him.

***

"Ari, I'm home," Rebecca called as she kicked the door closed behind her.

Her roommate, Ariela Horowitz, appeared from her bedroom dressed in yoga pants and a cami and took the pizza box from her. "Perfect timing. I'm starving."

"They charged me four dollars extra for the gluten-free crust."

"I'll pay you back." Ari lifted a slice of warm, gooey, veggie-topped pizza and folded it in half before taking a bite. "This is heaven."

Rebecca grabbed a plate from the kitchen and handed it to Ari. "Please, use this. I don't want a huge mess to clean up afterward."

"Fine." She took the plate with a huff and plopped down on the sofa. Both of them had grown up in wealthy families that employed several maids, but Ari still acted like they had one to pick up after them in the apartment they shared.

Instead, that job fell to Becca in exchange for living there rent-free.

She placed a slice on a plate for herself and joined her best friend on the sofa. "Why do you always insist on getting everything gluten-free? You're not allergic to it."

"I know, but it makes me bloat." Ari patted a perfectly flat stomach that would make a Victoria's Secret model envious. Petite, blond, and practically flawless, Ari was the embodiment of what an Upper East Side twenty-something should be.

"Whatever." Becca bit into the pizza, methodically chewing through the rubbery crust and wishing it was real bread. But since Ari had launched the "gluten is evil" campaign in their apartment, she had noticed her clothes were fitting a bit looser.

After a few minutes, Ari went back into the kitchen for another slice. "You're awfully quiet tonight."

"My mind is elsewhere." *Mainly on that moody, sullen, sexier-than-sin guy I gave my number to and wishing that he would call for non-NA things.*

"Work?"

That drew a derisive snort from her. Becca was an

editorial assistant at *Moderne* magazine, a periodical totally devoted to the selfie generation. "Hardly. Instead of giving me the go-ahead for my human trafficking article, they asked me to research the best places to have sex in public."

"Dressing rooms, first thing in the morning," Ari replied with a wink. "Then what is it? Something happen at your meeting?"

"You can say that." She forced herself to swallow the last bite and set her plate on the ottoman. "I got asked to help out this new guy until he can choose a sponsor."

Ari wrinkled her nose. "Does that mean you'll have to spend time with some strung-out user?"

Becca drew a sharp breath in through her nostrils and stiffened her spine. "Hello? That was me a few years ago."

"That's not what I meant."

"Then what *do* you mean?"

Ari had the decency to squirm on her side of the sofa and hugged one of the throw pillows. "It's just that, even when you were bad, you still functioned. Well, until the night of the Tribeca Ball. But, you know, you still looked normal."

"And you think I'm an exception to what a 'normal' addict should look like?"

"Well, you see all those people on the street begging for money so they can go out and get high…"

Becca got up and took her plate to the kitchen. After giving it a quick rinse in the sink and placing it in the dishwasher, she turned around to find Ari leaning against the wall with her lower lip jutted out in an apologetic pout.

"Sorry, Becca. It's just that I wish there was some

support group you could go to that was filled with people more like us. I'd worry less."

"I'm not going to get mugged or stabbed or whatever you're worried about there." She took Ari's plate and added it to the dishwasher. "Besides, Gary personally asked me help this guy because he thought I would know best where he was coming from."

Ari pushed off the wall, her worry changing into curiosity. "What is he? Some kind of Wall Street broker?"

"Not even close." Everything about Ethan screamed bad boy, from the tattoos peeking out from under his shirtsleeves to the way he tore down the street on his bike. "But I have to trust Gary's judgment and see where it goes."

"I saw that look." Ari flipped the dishwasher closed and moved to within a few inches of her, bumping hips with her. "You think he's hot."

Becca's cheeks heated as she wrapped up the leftover pizza. She remembered all the little details about him with heart-jolting clarity. The heat from his body. The scent that rose from his skin. The air of pure masculinity that surrounded him. "He's not bad looking."

"Uh-huh," Ari drawled, following close behind her. Ari wasn't going to leave her alone until she'd reported everything she could about Ethan.

Time to call uncle or I'll never hear the end of it. "What do you want to know?"

"What was he wearing?"

"Worn jeans that clung in all the right places, white T-shirt with an open red button-down shirt over it, black leather boots."

"Ass?"

The heat from her cheeks flowed lower to the pit of her stomach. "Nice and tight."

"Eyes?"

"Gray." And angry, like thunderclouds.

"Hair?"

"It looked black."

"What do you mean, it *looked* black? Was he wearing a hat or something?"

Becca shook her head. "It was really short, like he'd just shaved it all off recently."

"Ew!" Ari wrinkled her nose and backed away. "Is he going bald or something?"

"Not that I could tell." In fact, she'd wanted to run her hands over the thick, dark stubble.

"Then is he like some G.I. Joe wanna-be?"

"Nope." She put the pizza in the fridge and walked out of the kitchen, leaving her friend behind.

But Ari wouldn't let up that easily. "Oh, I see it now. Let me guess. Tattoos?"

"Yep."

"Piercings?"

"Nope."

"Motorcycle?"

"Ducati Streetfighter 848."

Ari's pale blond ponytail whipped her in the face as she shook her head. "No way, Becca. He's got 'stay away' written all over him."

"I know, but that's what makes him so fascinating." But it was more than the "angry at the world to cover up the pain" vibe she'd seen in his eyes. She couldn't shake the feeling that she knew him from somewhere.

"Your dad would have a stroke if you brought him home for dinner."

"Precisely, which is why he'll remain forbidden fruit as far as the romance department goes. Besides, I'm just going to help initiate him into the program until he has his own sponsor—someone he can call when he's in a crisis."

"And what if that crisis is a desperate need for a hookup?"

"Please, I do have some integrity. The guy looks like he's trying hard just to stay clean, and there's a reason why relationships are a no-no this early in the recovery process." But if she'd met him at a club, she'd have no problem hooking up with him. Ethan got her pulse racing in all the right ways. Dark, dangerous, and mysterious. She couldn't wait to unravel his story.

That is, if he ever trusted her enough to share it.

"Fine, but if he calls, make sure you check in with me so I know where you are." Ari stretched. "I'd better give Gabe a call before turning in. And speaking of brothers, Jacob called to find out if you were going to celebrate Rosh Hashanah with your parents. He'd come in from New Haven if you were."

"You both know I'm not." Part of staying clean involved avoiding situations where she'd be tempted to use again, and dealing with her father always triggered the desire to find the nearest dime bag.

"It's your life." Ari gave an indifferent shrug, but the look on her face said she'd be bringing it up again. "You still up for a little jog in the morning?"

Becca fought back a groan. A little jog with Ari equated

to three miles of sprinting through Central Park. "Can I take a pass?"

"Sure, and your thighs can get flabbier for it."

This time, Becca didn't hold back. A full-blown groan of pain was followed by a whimper when she imagined how her thighs would burn afterward. "Fine, I'll come."

"Good choice. We'll be leaving at five sharp."

Talk about torture. "Where do you get your energy, and can I borrow some of it?"

"Spend energy to make energy. See you in the morning." Ari pulled out her phone and was dialing her brother's number as she disappeared into her bedroom.

Becca plumped the pillows on the sofa before retreating to her own bedroom. Even though she'd severed ties with her family, she still managed to live a very comfortable life. The newly renovated two-bedroom apartment had sleek, modern lines that made them the envy of their peers. The view was spectacular, the security exceptional, and the rent was to die for. The Upper East Side apartment building belonged to Ari's grandmother, which meant they both got to live there rent-free. Becca's room was the smaller of the two, but even it had a walk-in closet and an attached bathroom.

She shed the dress she'd gotten at H&M and tossed it in the hamper before slipping into a pair of comfortable boxers and a cami. As she sat in bed with her notebook and pen, trying to come up with some places for the article, her mind kept drifting back to Ethan. Once again, the sense that she knew him hit her, but she had no idea why. He definitely didn't look like anyone who would've run in her circles growing up. But still, there was something about him...

She chucked her notebook across the room and fell back on her pillows. If she wanted to get anything done this next week, she needed to stop obsessing over a guy she just met.

A guy who was trying to stay clean.

A guy who acted like he wanted nothing to do with her.

Time for some mind-cleansing music. She scrolled through the music on her iPod Shuffle until she came to one of her favorite Ravinia's Rejects songs. Unlike the driving rock beats of their other songs, this one was slow and quiet, the acoustic guitars melding with the perfect harmonies of the two lead singers. During her first days of sobriety, she'd listened to the song over and over until it haunted her dreams. She closed her eyes and let the music wash over her. The chorus came on, and she sang along with it, letting each word soothe her soul.

One day at a time
One wish on every star that makes the heavens shine
One more heartbeat until I know that I'm fine
Just need to take it one day at a time.

When the song ended, she took a cleansing breath and turned off her light.

Just take it one day at a time.

Chapter Two

Ethan strummed his guitar, but the chords formed a dissonant mishmash that resembled anything but music. In the past, when he'd hit a wall, he'd always shoot up and find inspiration in the dreamlike high he'd gotten from the heroin. The notes would dance in front of him like mirages from a muse, and his fingers would glide over the strings as though they were divinely controlled.

So very different from the hours he'd spent that afternoon with a stack of blank sheet music in front of him.

A zing shot up his arm, followed by the familiar craving. He flexed his fingers, trying to shake it, but it wound even tighter around his arm and crawled into his chest. *Just one more hit to get the music flowing again.*

The ring of his phone jerked him away from the siren song. He checked the number before answering. "Hi, Mom."

"Hello, Ethan. How are you doing?"

"The same." *No better, no worse.*

"Are you going to your meeting tonight?"

Shit. He'd forgotten that the NA meeting was tonight.

"Probably."

"Well, shouldn't you be on your way now?"

He checked the time. Twenty minutes until it started. Just enough time to hop on his bike and find parking somewhere near the church. It would be faster to take the subway, but the risk of someone spotting him was too great. And taxis were ridiculous in the city. "I guess so."

"Ethan…" Usually, when his mom drawled out his name, it was a warning. But this time, it was more of a plea. Even though getting and staying clean was his own battle, she wanted to be his ally. She'd flown to LA the minute she'd heard of Ty's death to help him through his grief and arranged the moving of his stuff to New York while he was in detox. But she also respected his boundaries enough not to nag him.

Still, the plea in her voice was enough of a guilt trip. He stood and grabbed his jacket. "I'm on my way now."

"Let me know if you need anything." The hesitation in her voice was something he wasn't used to. As a former lawyer, his mother had always been one to cut directly to the point. But like Adam and the rest of his brothers, she was treading carefully around him. Probably terrified that one word would send him over the deep end.

Irritation crawled up his spine. They thought he was weak and fragile. But he'd prove them wrong. "Thanks, Mom. I'm fine."

"I'm glad to hear that." The tone of her voice revealed she didn't quite believe him.

"Got to go, Mom. I don't want to be late." He hung up before her doubt infected him.

His loft in Hell's Kitchen didn't have a parking garage,

but it did have a freight elevator that was big enough to accommodate him and his bike. When he got to the street, he hopped on and wove through the Midtown streets until he came to the old church that housed the meetings. Parking was easier to find tonight, but instead of going inside, he lingered on his bike with his helmet on. The motor rumbled underneath him. The craving to surrender to his muse rather than fight it rebounded in his moment of hesitation. He gripped the throttle, revving it up in tempo to the rising frustration in his gut.

Then someone knocked on his helmet.

He snapped his head around to find Rebecca standing on the sidewalk beside him. She held on to the strap of her messenger bag with both hands, but the unyielding stance of her legs told him she wasn't leaving until he acknowledged her.

He lifted his visor. "Don't you know better than to walk up to strangers and assault them?"

"First off, you're not a stranger. Second, I tried calling your name before I tapped on your helmet. I'd hardly call that assault."

The craving dissipated along with his anger. He turned off the motor and pulled off his helmet. "What made you so certain it was me?"

"I recognized your bike." Her gaze drifted over the Ducati in an amorous way that made his dick envious. What he wouldn't give to have her look at him that way. "A 2014 Ducati Streetfighter 848. A 132-horsepower Testastretta engine. Six-speed transmission." She bit her bottom lip and sucked in a deep breath through her nose. "Beautiful."

A Seductive Melody

He grew hard just from listening to her. Did she have any idea how much hearing her recite the technical specs of the bike turned him on?

Her gaze turned back to him. "Are you coming?"

Ms. Park Avenue intrigued him enough to make him nod. "Wouldn't miss it."

But when he got inside, he found himself as bored as he was last week. The only thing that kept him glued to his seat was the woman sitting next to him. She listened to every person who shared, her face softening in empathy as they whined about their individual trials and tribulations. *What makes an uptown girl like her care about the everyday suffering of recovering addicts?*

She was a riddle he longed to solve. Her textured short-sleeved sweater dress screamed designer label, yet the heels of her boots were well worn. The way she unclipped her dark hair and removed the dangling earrings at the start of the meeting seemed to be part of some evening unwinding ritual, much like she would do when she came home from work. Her messenger bag with the laptop inside made her appear to have some sort of professional job, but he had no idea what field. The little details he gleaned from studying her whetted his curiosity and made him wish the meeting would end soon so he could start asking her questions.

When Gary finally called them to form a circle for the closing prayer, a twinge of panic rooted itself in his chest. He curled his fingers in his palm to keep it from spreading. *What if she tries to back out on me?*

But after they adjourned, she smiled up at him. "So, you made it through your second NA meeting."

Barely.

"I think I promised you coffee."

"And information about yourself."

Rebecca tilted her head to the side, her brows furrowed in a quizzical way. "Sure, if that's what you want, but if you'd rather talk about how you're doing—"

"I don't."

Both brows rose in response, erasing the lines between them, but she didn't pry any further. "I know a nice little Viennese café a few blocks from here."

"Sounds good." He grabbed his helmet and followed her outside.

Once they'd crossed the first street, she turned and asked, "Have you had dinner?"

"No." Small talk like this he could handle. He just hoped she wouldn't take it as an invitation to start asking about his personal life.

"I highly recommend their sandwiches. Or their soups." She stared down at the sidewalk, her lips twitching in a shy grin. "But the desserts are to die for."

So, Ms. Park Avenue had a sweet tooth. "Good to know."

Her eyes widened like a child's in a toy store when they entered the café. She went straight to the dessert case and licked her lips. "You have the Sacher-torte today."

"I made it this morning in the hopes you'd come by, Becca," a middle-aged woman with a slight German accent behind the counter said. "Shall I cut you a slice?"

Rebecca nodded. "And could you give me another slice to go, too, Gitta?"

"Expecting a rough week at work?"

"Horrendous," she replied with a laugh.

"And I take it you'd like your usual drink?"

Rebecca nodded again. "I'm so predictable."

So far, she'd seemed to be anything but predictable to him. But he was willing to watch and learn.

Gitta turned to him. "And for your friend?"

"Just coffee," he replied. Anything more might overwhelm him.

"I'll bring it to your table in a minute." Gitta turned to start steaming some milk.

Rebecca took his hand to lead him to a table, but the gentle touch managed to kick the air from his lungs. He'd lived so long in a world where most women begged permission to touch him that her complete indifference to his celebrity status shocked him. But then, maybe that was a good thing. If she didn't know who he was, he might be able to let his guard down long enough to enjoy coffee with her.

He glanced around the room, but no one was staring at them or whispering to their friends while pointing at him. No flash of a paparazzo's camera. No cringe-worthy fear that sharing dessert with Rebecca would be tomorrow's headline on TMZ.

For the first time in years, he felt almost normal.

He placed his helmet in an empty chair and sat down across from her. As much as he wanted to relax, he couldn't quite let his guard down. "Come here often?"

"Is it that obvious?"

"Just slightly."

She laughed at his dry reply. "You're really missing out on Gitta's Sacher-torte. It was her grandmother's recipe."

"I haven't been very hungry lately."

She nodded, empathy flittering across her features. "Yeah, once you've had your guts turned inside out for a week, it takes a while for the appetite to come back."

He leaned forward, elbows on the table, and lowered his voice. "I still have a hard time believing someone like you understands what I'm going through."

"Why?"

Her quick reply caught him off guard. He backed away and gestured to her appearance. "Because..."

"Because I don't look the part?"

Before he could answer, Gitta interrupted them by setting a plate of chocolate cake and two mugs on the table. Steam rose from his mug of black coffee, but a mound of cinnamon-sprinkled whipped cream covered her beverage. "What is that?"

She stirred some of the cream into her drink and licked the spoon. "Cinnamon hazelnut hot chocolate."

"Someone's going to have a sugar rush tonight."

She flashed him a wicked grin before drinking a gulp of her hot chocolate. When she lowered her mug, a dot of whipped cream lay perched on the end of her nose.

Ethan tried to smother the laugh that rose from his throat, but it was no use. Instead, he let it out and reached for a napkin. "You have a little something on your nose."

"Oh?" But instead of acting mortified and reaching for a mirror like he expected her to do, she laughed with him and wiped her nose with a napkin. "Got it?"

He nodded, once again surprised by her. Here was a refined young woman who wasn't the least bit concerned with her appearance. Very different from the high-society girls he'd gone to high school with or the models and actresses he'd met through the years.

She took a more cautious sip this time. "I'd promised to be an open book to you, so ask away."

He crossed his arms and sat back in his chair, watching her nibble at the cake. So many things about her intrigued him. Where did he begin? But one question always lingered in the back of his mind. "How long have you been clean?"

"Two years and a hundred and fifty days." she replied without looking up from her cake. "At least, this time around."

"You relapsed?" She seemed so calm and collected that he wouldn't have expected that from her.

"Yep. The first time, I was forced into rehab by my parents. Suboxone and all that mess. It didn't take me long to figure out how to hide my pills and go back to the good stuff again."

"So what made you stop?"

"I OD'd and almost died." She kept eating her cake as though she were talking about a boring day at work instead of a near-death experience. "At a big charity ball, no less. The press had a field day with that one."

"And why was that?"

That made her pause and look up from her plate. She held his gaze long enough for him to realize her eyes were more green than blue today. "You remember what I said last week about us taking the 'anonymous' part seriously."

"Yes."

Her chin quivered, and she swallowed hard. "Then let's leave it at that."

Another layer of mystery to her. Whoever Rebecca was, she was famous enough to be known by the press. "Fine. Then my next question—what do you do?"

"I'm an assistant at a women's magazine," she said with a roll of her eyes.

"Not your dream job?"

"Not even close, but it's a foot in the door."

"For what? Fashion?"

"No." She didn't expand, turning her attention instead on the remaining crumbs of her Sacher-torte as she engaged her fork in a repetitive dance of stab, smash, and scrape. "Next question."

"Are you seeing anyone?" he blurted out before he realized what he was saying.

The corners of her mouth rose, and she looked up at him through her lashes. "Why do you want to know?"

Shit! Not the way he wanted this conversation to go. It was one thing to stick to safe, NA-related topics, but if he found out she was single, he'd have a hard time keeping his thoughts clean around her. "Um, because I'd like to make sure some jealous boyfriend isn't going to hunt me down and punch me for calling you in the middle of the night."

Her smile widened into something both teasing and inviting. "No danger of that."

No danger why? Because she's single? Or because she has a really understanding significant other?

Time to steer the conversation back to safe subjects before he gave into temptation and invited her back to his place. "What changed between the first time and the second time?"

A Seductive Melody

"It was my choice." She pushed her plate aside and leaned forward. "I think that was the most important thing that helped me stay clean. I'm not doing this because I was forced to by my parents or the law or some other external means. I'm doing this for me. Everything I need is in here." She patted the area over her heart.

An ache formed in the center of his chest. He resisted the urge to mirror her and press the heel of his hand against his ribs to ease the pain. He'd been the one who'd decided to give up heroin, but there was still a voice in the back of his mind telling him he'd end up just like Ty. "And what if that's not enough?"

"Then you look for little daily victories. For example—not embarrassing your friends or family. Or not wondering where your money went because you basically handed it over to your dealer. Or not waking up next to some stranger you dragged home while you were high."

He nodded with each example she'd given, knowing firsthand how those situations felt—until she got to the next one.

"Or not having to give up open-toed shoes."

"Open-toed shoes?" It was so ridiculous, a laugh wedged itself between his words. "What the hell does that have to do with staying clean?"

A blush stole up into her cheeks, and she slid her gaze to the side. "It's kind of embarrassing."

"You said you were an open book, and that I'd understand you better than most."

"True." She bit her lip and squirmed in her seat like he'd just asked her to reveal the color of her underwear. "The first time I went into rehab, it was because my stepmother noticed the track marks on my arms. So when I relapsed, I got more creative with where I shot up. You won't believe how quickly you can get high from shooting up between your toes."

He nodded, finally seeing what she meant. "So your parents weren't suspicious because all they saw were flawless arms."

She glanced up at him through her lashes. "Yeah, it worked for several months until…"

"Until you OD'd," he finished almost in a whisper. His throat tightened, choking him as he asked, "How close did you come to dying?"

"I had broken ribs from the CPR that was done to keep me alive until the medics arrived with Narcan."

Her answer was honest, direct, lacking the coyness from earlier. But it didn't release the invisible rope of guilt squeezing around his neck and chest. How is it she survived when his best friend didn't? If he'd managed to find Ty sooner—if he'd acted on the signs that Ty was slipping further and further under the spell of heroin and not caring how much he took as long as he got high—would his best friend still be here today? If he'd just watched him closer, taken away his needles, would it have made a difference?

If he'd accepted Ty's invitation to go back to his apartment that night to get high with him, would things have turned out differently? Would he have been able to call 911 and save him like the medics had done with Rebecca? Or would he have followed his best friend like he'd always done, even into death?

He squeezed his eyes shut to block out all the scenarios

racing through his mind, but the guilt didn't ease. And the only solution he could find was in the seductive voice inside that beckoned him to relapse into his old habits. One hit was all he'd need to quiet the anguish, the doubt, the pain.

Sweat beaded along his hairline as he battled the familiar demons. Panic raced along his veins like an electrical current, setting every nerve on edge. He balled his hands into fists, fighting the growing urge to give in.

And then a cool hand covered his, pulling him from the whirlpool that threatened to drag him under.

He opened his eyes to find Rebecca watching him with worry etched around the corners of her normally smiling mouth. A sober sense of understanding laced her words as she said, "I know it's hard, but don't give in to it, Ethan."

He yanked his hand back. "What the fuck do you know?"

"I've been there, remember?" She retreated to her side of the table. "Tell me what just happened, and maybe I can help you through it."

It rankled his insides that she thought he needed her help. He alone was the one who'd decided to come clean. He'd made it through detox alone. And he'd be able to overcome the craving alone, too. "I don't have to tell you anything."

He fished a few bills out of his wallet and threw them on the table before grabbing his helmet and stomping out the door. He was done with this crap.

"Stop it right there," a stern female voice called after him.

He drew to a stop a split second before Rebecca

grabbed his shoulder and spun him around. "What is your problem?" she asked, her body rigid with anger.

"Maybe you're my problem."

"That's bullshit and you know it." She rammed her finger into the center of his chest as she drove each point home, backing him into the alley between the café and its neighbor. "You're so angry at the world that you're willing to blame everyone for your problems but yourself."

He'd been brought up to never strike a woman, but she came pretty damned close to pushing enough of his buttons to make him consider shoving her out of his way. Instead, he drew up every inch of his height so he towered over her and dropped his voice to issue a low, sinister warning. "And that's where you're wrong."

But instead of cowering, she held her ground, her face inches from his. "Then prove it."

Intimidation wasn't working with her, and for the wildest second, he fought the urge to kiss her. Maybe that would shock her enough to leave him alone. But he kept his arms at his sides, his eyes locked in the staring match they'd entered. "You first."

"Fine. I don't know what your story is because you won't share it with me, but Gary knew enough about you to think I'd be able to help, and I trust his judgment."

"You want me to open up, and yet you purposely evaded several of my questions in there. How do you expect me to trust you when you obviously don't trust me?" He turned on his heel and made it three steps before she called out his name. His mind told him to keep walking, but something else made him halt.

"You're right," she said, and his defenses cracked. He'd

been so ready to say the hell with this, but with two little words, she'd managed to temper the rage boiling inside him.

She approached him slowly, circling around him at arm's reach like she expected him to take a swing at her if she got too close. Her face remained wary as she studied him. "Can I trust you?"

He drew a breath into his lungs and held it while he weighed the cost of listening to another word from her. So far, she'd managed to get under his skin more than any other woman he'd ever known—in both good ways and bad ways. And if he opened the door to her, she'd keep invading his personal life until she knew all his secrets.

But if he held one of her secrets, he could use it as leverage for when she got too close.

"You can trust me."

She glanced over her shoulder at the pedestrians on the sidewalk behind them before pushing even further into the alley. The smell of rotting garbage wafted around them, but she seemed oblivious to it. "Have you heard of Shore Hotels?"

"Who hasn't?" He'd stayed in his fair share of the luxury hotel chain's rooms when he was touring.

"My great-grandfather started them."

"You're Becca Shore?" Her confession set off a chain of recognition that unfolded like a clap of thunder. Images of a blond, tanned, partying heiress who frequently graced the tabloids a few years ago flashed before him. They seemed so at odds with the calm woman in front of him, but when he looked closer, he recognized her face. It was a bit fuller, and she'd traded the bronzed glow for a flawless ivory complexion, but the eyes were the same.

She ran her fingers through her dark hair, one side of her mouth quirking up in a half smile. "Would you like to see my driver's license?"

"No, I believe you." And more important, he finally understood why Gary had suggested she help him out until he had a sponsor. If anyone knew about trying to stay clean while under the pressures of fame, it would be her. "So what happened to you?"

She flipped her hair over her shoulder, her spine stiffening. "Excuse me?"

"I mean, I couldn't open up a gossip rag without reading something about you, and then—*bam!*—you disappeared. What happened to the army of paparazzi that used to follow you around and catch you with your underwear missing?"

"After I OD'd, I purposely made sure I disappeared for a while so I could get my shit together. I checked into a treatment center. By the time I left there, I started caring less about what others thought of me and more about what I thought of myself. I changed my appearance, finished school, got a job, all while flying under the radar." She shrugged. "It's kind of nice to be normal for a change."

"But you're still a Shore."

"Yeah, but I'm so boring now, the press leaves me alone. Besides, I don't think they'd recognize me. You didn't."

But did she recognize him? He searched for any sign of recognition, but saw nothing. Either she was completely clueless or completely unfazed by his celebrity status. It didn't matter, judging by the way his shoulders unknotted after learning who she was. Even if she did know, he doubted she'd go blabbing to the press about him.

"So does that help you any?" she asked.

"Loads."

"Then I'll see you next week?"

"Maybe." Time to leave before she started prying into his personal life again.

She caught his arm and stopped him. "Please."

Such a simple word, and yet it was strange to witness a wealthy heiress say it. "Why?"

"Because I want to help you any way I can. But I can't unless you let me. Even if the meetings aren't your thing, I'm still here if you need someone to talk to." She released his arm and took a step back toward the café. "I'd better go retrieve that slice of Sacher-torte before someone else does."

Part of him longed to follow her back into the café and spill his guts to her over another slice of cake, but both fear and pride held him back. He wasn't ready to trust her.

Not yet.

But he would be willing to consider taking her out for coffee again next week, if only to hear more about how she managed to dodge the press all these years and move on with her life.

Chapter Three

Becca drummed her pen on her thigh as she stood against the wall in the conference room. It was Monday, the day when the editor-in-chief of *Moderne* magazine, Elaine Halpern, listened to story ideas from her staff and either approved them or shot them down. As an assistant, Becca was required to take notes and research the articles for the staff writers. She wasn't allowed to pitch story ideas.

But that didn't stop her.

"How about a story on how the VA is falling short on women's health issues?" she asked.

Elaine shook her head. "Too serious for our readers. Next."

Becca gritted her teeth and zoned out. Everything she suggested was "too dark" or "too serious" for their readers. What kind of demographics were they catering to, anyway? Based on the insipid material she was asked to research each week, she wondered if their readers cared about anything other than fashion and sex.

"That sounds like a great idea, Hilde. Rebecca can look up some info for you."

A Seductive Melody

Her attention snapped back to the meeting the second she heard Elaine say her name. Too bad she missed what she was supposed to research. She tried to stay focused as the writers tossed out a few more ideas before the meeting ended, her mind growing more numb with each one that was approved. *Why couldn't I have gotten a job with* Time *or* Newsweek? *Why* Moderne?

Because it was the only place that offered me a job.

Everyone else still saw her as Becca Shore, the strung-out party girl. Just another obstacle to overcome on the way to becoming a respected journalist.

Her morning latte mingled with her bitterness to form an acid that gnawed at the inside of her stomach. She closed her eyes and focused on the positives before the bitterness erupted into a "fuck it all" scene.

I've got one foot in the door, which is better than where I was before.

I'm gaining insight into how the magazine publishing world works.

I'm making contacts and building my resume.

I can use this experience to help me later.

A Zen-like sensation surrounded her with each positive thought, followed by a calm acceptance. It was only the sound of her name that pulled her back to reality.

Hilde, one of the staff writers, stood in front of her. She was sleek and sophisticated in her late thirties, her hair perfectly highlighted and never out of place, and her face showed the benefits of her regular Botox injections. The meeting had adjourned, and the other writers were filing out the room. "Sleeping on the job?"

"No, just brainstorming ideas."

"Good, because I'll need your help." Hilde beckoned her to follow her out of the conference room. "By the way, you have some balls pitching story ideas as an assistant."

"I have to start somewhere," she replied with a shrug. "It's not like I'm going to get fired for suggesting something."

"But it's not scoring you any points with the other writers."

Becca glanced around the office and caught a couple of disapproving glares that backed Hilde's warning. "What are they worried about? It's not like Elaine ever accepts any of my ideas anyway."

"Just offering you a piece of friendly advice." Hilde leaned in and lowered her voice. "Between you and me, though, I find your ideas thought provoking, even if they aren't right for this magazine. You keep searching for good stories like that, maybe you can end up at a place that appreciates your enthusiasm."

If only...

"You mean you don't appreciate me now?" she teased back.

"I'll appreciate you even more if you can help me research these topics." She flipped open her notebook. "Article one: How to take the perfect selfie."

Becca bit back a groan and scribbled the topic down. "I'm on it."

"Great, and when you're done with that, you can help me with the article on holiday makeup trends. But first, I'd love a latte from downstairs. You know how I like it." Hilde walked off without another word.

Becca clenched her shoulder blades together and repeated her positives list from earlier before heading down to the coffee stand.

Once she fetched the venti, double-shot, nonfat, sugar-free vanilla latte with no foam for Hilde, Becca settled into her cubicle and popped her ear buds in. Music from her iPod Shuffle filled her ears and drowned out the chatter around her. A search of the Internet found tons of tips on taking selfies and plunged her into a world of camera angles, expressions, filters, and cropping techniques.

She was nearing the end of what she hoped would be enough information when the hard, driving beat of one of Ravinia's Rejects' songs came on. She sat back and bobbed her head in time with the music and was instantly transported back to the carefree days where she'd dance all night to songs like it at a club, drink in hand, one hit away from bliss.

The familiar craving flared in the back of her mind. No matter how long she'd been clean, she'd always remember how good it felt to get high. She curled her fingers around the armrests of her chair until the craving faded. Thankfully, tonight was her NA meeting. Just knowing it existed helped her push past the memory and move forward.

The song was ending by the time her fingers were back on the keyboard, but instead of continuing to research her article, she entered "Ravinia's Rejects" into the search field. At the top of the list were articles about the tragic death of the lead guitarist, Tyler Bransford, last month. Most of the news out there speculated that the band had broken up, but there was still talk about them releasing some of the material they'd been recording when he died.

She clicked on one of the articles citing the cause of death as a heroin overdose, and her breath left her in a mournful sigh. Such a waste of talent. She followed it up with a prayer of thanks that she hadn't suffered the same fate and continued reading.

The article mentioned that Ethan Kelly, the lead singer, had checked into a rehab facility shortly after Ty's death and hadn't been seen since. She stared at his picture, noting his long black hair and stormy gray eyes, and was struck by the nagging sensation that he looked familiar. At first, she laughed it off since she'd been a fan of the band since their debut album, but the more she looked at the picture, the stronger the sensation became.

She clicked on the picture to enlarge it. A knot twisted her stomach, and the hair on her arms rose. A few clicks later, she'd loaded the picture into an editing program and removed his hair. Her breath hitched when she saw the man scowling back at her on the screen.

Shit!

No wonder Gary had asked her to be Ethan's sponsor.

He was Ethan Kelly.

***

Becca hurried down the crowded sidewalk, the butterflies still fluttering in her stomach hours later. It was one thing to know she'd been asked to sponsor a man who needed help. It was another thing when the man was a rock god she'd worshipped since she was a teenager.

Please don't let me turn into a blathering idiot around him.

It wasn't like she hadn't rubbed shoulders with celebrities before. She'd grown up surrounded by actors, designers, models, and musicians. But with a few exceptions, they were mostly her parents' friends, not hers. And even during her party days, she'd never actually met someone she completely idolized.

Get over it, Becca. You're not a teenager anymore. Besides, if you fawn all over him like some crazed fan, he'll run away and relapse.

That stopped her in her tracks. More than anything, she needed to watch what she said and how she acted around him. He'd been so closed off about himself. If he even caught a whiff that she knew who he was, he'd be gone before she could stop him. And if he ended up like his band mate...

Guilt quieted her giddiness and sobered her to the reality of the situation. She'd been in his shoes. She knew what it was like to want to disappear from the press long enough to get herself together. And she would support his decision to do the same.

She resumed the quick pace of her fellow New Yorkers, focusing instead on ways to reassure Ethan his secret was safe with her without bringing it up. When she got to the church where the meetings were held, she turned to go inside without paying any attention to the streets around her.

"Hey, Bec," a man called from the curb.

She spun around to find Ethan still straddling his motorcycle, even though the engine was off. He pulled off his helmet and approached her. "I was waiting for you."

"Y–you were?" she stuttered, and a wave of heat rose along the back of her neck. She locked her knees to keep from swooning like some silly fan-girl. *Geez, Becca, snap out of it.*

The smile he gave her did little to slow the frantic beating of her heart. He'd always seemed dangerous. A little rough around the edges. But that one rare flash of his pearly whites turned her insides to goo. "I don't dare go in there alone."

"Oh, yeah." He was just interested in her as a support system, not as anything more. After the disappointment ebbed, she realized that was probably a good thing. Knowing the boundaries that were in place would keep her from crossing the lines.

But as she got a full view of the way his jeans molded his ass, her thoughts went from responsible sponsor to lust-filled woman. Even if he weren't a bad-boy rock star, she'd still love to get him out of those jeans. Still, she needed to put that aside. If she could get over heroin, she could certainly keep her desire for Ethan Kelly in check.

"Nice parking spot," she quipped in an attempt to keep the mood light.

"Lucked out," he replied without turning back.

And they were back to the minimal responses. Perhaps it was for the best.

The meeting was shorter than usual tonight since Gary had brought in a speaker. Not that she was paying much attention. Ethan was proving to be too much of a distraction. She'd been around some of the sexiest men alive like Ari's brother, Gabe, but none of them left her on edge like Ethan did.

She sat straighter in her chair, trying to keep her attention on the speaker instead of the man sitting next to her. *It's all because he's someone you've admired for years, and you haven't gotten laid in four months. Just a bad combination of a crush and a dry spell. Nothing more.*

Then she made the mistake of glancing at him out of the corner of her eye. He was watching her with that intense, brooding gaze that made her nipples harden.

But damn, what a fantasy that would be to spend the night with him.

She turned away with an exasperated sigh and did her best to ignore him for the rest of the meeting. By the time Gary got back on the podium to thank the speaker, she'd almost forgotten about Ethan.

Of course, that would be the moment he chose to rush out of the room.

Damn it! She offered an apologetic smile to Gary and chased after Ethan.

He was already on his bike and strapping on his helmet by the time she caught up to him.

"What's the rush?" she asked.

"I don't do prayer." He revved up the engine in an angry growl that added emphasis to the angst underlying his reply.

This she could handle. She'd spent most of the week preparing to handle the angry Ethan, and putting her plan into action was just what she needed to clear out the haze of desire. "Fair enough."

He released the throttle and tilted his head to the side. "What? No questions? No trying to get me to reveal why?"

She shook her head. Last week had taught her that he'd only volunteer information when he was ready. Questions only made things worse. But now she understood why.

He sat back on his bike, his brows drawing together

like she'd just stumped him.

Thirty seconds of uneasy silence passed between them before she proceeded to the next step in her plan. "I'm going to get some cake and coffee. You're welcome to join me."

She turned to go toward Gitta's café when a gloved hand grabbed her wrist.

"I can give you a ride," he offered. "That is, if you're not too scared."

She chuckled. "What makes you think that?"

"I like to go fast." Behind his challenge lay a hint of flirtation.

A delicious tingle rippled up her spine. "So do I."

"Prove it." He reached behind him for the spare helmet and shoved it in her hands.

She chewed her bottom lip while she ran her hands over the smooth fiberglass. Could she keep it together while they whipped through the streets of Manhattan, her arms wrapped around his waist, her thighs gripping his? Talk about the ultimate foreplay, even if it was only for a few blocks.

But on the other hand, if she could get him to join her at the café, then maybe she could also make some headway on his recovery. She slipped the helmet on. "You're on."

A minute later, she had secured her messenger bag across her chest and climbed onto the seat behind him. Even through the thick leather of his jacket, she could feel his lean, hard muscles.

"Hold on," he shouted a split second before pulling out into traffic.

A Seductive Melody

The speed awakened the long-dormant sense of exhilaration she'd buried years ago when she'd given up her wild lifestyle. She resisted the urge to raise her arms in the air and shout with joy. Instead, she kept her arms wrapped tightly around his waist, leaning her body from side to side as they weaved through the lanes. The cool autumn air cut through her clothes as they sped along the street, and she nuzzled closer to him, drawing in the warm scents of cologne and leather. The ride would be over before she wanted it to end, but for those few precious moments, she savored the freedom he offered her.

***

Ethan's groin throbbed by the time he pulled into a parking spot near the café. What the fuck had he been thinking, inviting Becca for a ride? It was bad enough that she kept ambushing his thoughts as he lay in bed every night. But to feel her body pressed against his, to witness the fearless way she accepted his challenge and rode with him, to hear the excited hitch of her breath with every turn—it all made him harder than a high school kid discovering porn for the first time.

She hopped off his bike and removed her helmet. The ride had tousled her hair so she looked more like a sex kitten, and another jolt of desire shot straight to his dick.

"That was fun," she said with a grin and handed the spare helmet back to him, "but next time, I'll drive and you can ride bitch."

"Like hell you will." He strapped the spare to the back of his bike, thankful for the few seconds the mindless task gave him to allow the ache in his crotch to lessen. By the time he was done, he could climb off his bike without wincing.

He found Becca drooling in front of the dessert case again when he entered the café. "So many yummy choices," she murmured.

"But I see they don't have your Sacher-torte tonight."

"Doesn't matter. There's still plenty to choose from." She pointed to a tray full of little pink square cakes. "*Punschkrapfen.*" Then to a cherry strudel. "*Weichselstrudel.*"

Her obvious love for desserts lifted the dark mood that had seized control of him during the meeting, and he caught himself laughing. "Why do I feel like I need to say *gesundheit* after each of those things?"

She elbowed him and gave him a wry smile before turning her attention back to the dessert case. "I think I'll go with the *Dobostorte* tonight."

"Very good," Gitta said from behind the counter. "And anything for you?"

"Just a coffee."

He joined Becca at a corner table that was hidden from most of the café, noting the way she craned her neck to check out the rest of the room behind him. "Have your whereabouts been discovered?" he teased.

"No, I was more worried about y—" Her mouth snapped shut, but not before he figured out the last word.

The muscles along his back locked. "And why would you be worried about me?"

She bit her lip and combed her fingers through her hair, never meeting his gaze. "You seem pretty protective of your privacy, that's all. And I want to make sure you can enjoy a cup of coffee without being disturbed."

The tension rounded his shoulder and spread to his

gut. "Is there something I need to know?"

The tone of his voice turned accusing, but if someone had told her who he was, he was done with this NA bullshit.

She finally looked at him with guileless blue-green eyes and slowly shook her head. "You know who I am, and you know how hard I guard my privacy. I just want to do the same for you."

His stomach unknotted, but he still couldn't completely relax. Something had changed from last week, and for a moment, he was tempted to ask her if she wanted to get back on his bike and ride until the sun came up. Even with the blue balls it threatened to give him, he preferred that over what hung in the air between them.

Gitta brought their order to their table, and Becca dove into her cake. "You didn't get anything to eat?"

"I'm not much of a sweets person."

"I could tell that, but I figured you might be game for the sour cherry strudel."

"Sour cherry?"

"Um-hmm," she said before she swallowed a mouthful of her cake. "You seem like the sour type."

So they were back with the teasing. "Do I? You, on the other hand, are definitely all about the sweet."

"As you can tell by my ass."

He leaned over to study the shape of her thighs and how they vanished into a very squeezable ass. "Nothing wrong with it as far as I can tell."

She choked on her whipped cream–topped hot chocolate. Her face reddened as she struggled to catch her breath. "Are you flirting with me?"

"Are you bothered by it?"

She didn't answer, but he caught a hint of a smile before she covered her mouth with her coffee mug. "How was your week?"

"It sucked." He expected her to ask him to elaborate or maybe try to tease out some details why it sucked, but she continued to watch him with the expectant arch of her eyebrows without saying a word.

When the silence stretched into a minute, the heat climbing along the base of his spine forced him to shift in his seat. He turned away before she saw how uneasy he'd become from such a simple question.

Sucked didn't begin to describe his week. Between struggling to find the music without giving in to his muse and dealing with the constant phone calls from his mother and older brother Adam, he could feel the cracks forming in his thin shell of sobriety. He couldn't sleep, not without waking up in a cold sweat and wishing he had a bag of Sweet Dreams. Instead, he was left with visions of finding his best friend wide-eyed in death with a needle still in his arm and a craving to make it all go away.

He ran his hand over the tattoo on his left arm and repeated, "It sucked."

"You're nearing the one-month mark, right?" After he nodded, she continued, "It's like a New Year's resolution, staying clean. Some people succeed, but most of us hit that first speed bump around the one-month mark. You go through the Super Flu and swear you will never touch the stuff that makes you feel so rotten ever again. You come out feeling renewed by this vow and empowered by whatever drove you to come clean. But little by little, the day-to-day pressure of reality begins to wear on you, and your resolve starts to crumble. The void you once filled with heroin becomes larger and larger until it consumes you. And around the one-month mark, you're faced with the choice of do I give in and get high, or do I find something else to fill the void?"

She had no idea how fucking accurate she was.

"All of us started using to fill that void, and it's different for each of us. But once you identify it, then you can come up with ways to fill it without getting high."

"I doubt sweets will do it for me."

She gave him a soft laugh that deflected the pessimistic sting of his words. "They don't do it for me, either."

"Then what does?"

She set her mug down and stared at the plate. Like last week, she engaged in the repetitive motions of stabbing, smashing, and scraping the cake crumbs with her fork. "For me, it was finding some sort of purpose for my life. I wanted to be more than a spoiled, airhead heiress."

"And are you now?"

"Depends." She looked across the table at him, the silent plea in her eyes echoing louder in his mind than any words she'd spoken.

Part of him wanted to bolt from the table, but the rest of him took some small comfort in knowing she understood what he was going through. No one else did. Not his friends. Not his family. Not his agent or producers. The only other person he'd reached out to was his younger brother's assistant, Sarah, and that was only because she knew the best places to go for detox.

But Becca had been there. She'd gone through this hell

and seemed to have her shit together now.

Unlike him.

A bead of sweat rolled down the side of his face, and he leaned forward on the table, his eyes lowered. "Where do I start?"

"At the beginning."

A single note of bitter laughter rose from his throat. "I started using because my best friend did, and I looked up to him."

He waited for her to mock him for being a lemming, but instead, she said in a choked voice, "And did he inspire you to come clean, too?"

"Yeah." Finding Ty dead was the cruelest form of wake-up call he'd ever experienced.

He glanced at her to gauge her reaction and found the same patient plea for him to continue.

They say confession is good for the soul....

He took a deep breath and opened his up to her. "I'd always been more of a dabbler, getting high here and there as needed. My best friend was more of a King Kong user, mixing his daily heroin with something else to achieve different highs. Sometimes it was as simple as smoking it with marijuana. Sometimes it was harder stuff like crack or PCP. Whatever was available at the moment. But until the last few weeks of his life, he still functioned. He showed up to work, and he never, ever bailed on me."

His voice caught as he added, "That is, until the one morning when he didn't show up."

He wasn't used to a woman with nothing to say, but Becca's silence rattled him to the core. No questions. No sounds of acceptance or judgment. No movement to or away from him. He had no clue how she was reacting to his story, and he refused to look up from the table to read her face. The frustration mounted inside until it finally erupted with a bang of his fist on the table.

"I was so fuckin' angry at him," he admitted. "He'd thrown his life away. Wasted the talent he'd been given. Destroyed everything we'd worked so hard for. At first, all I could feel was rage. Then this ache followed, like he'd taken some part of me with him. And God, it hurt."

He pressed his hand against the center of his chest where the emptiness still lingered. "Once I experienced that pain, that anger, that sense of abandonment..."

He shook his head as though it would clear the dark emotions swirling inside. Visions of his mother and brothers going through the same hell filled his head like they had in the days following Ty's death. "I never wanted anyone I cared about to go through that."

"So you found a reason to get clean," she said at last.

It wasn't a question, but he still nodded.

"Then keep holding on to that." She reached into her purse to pull out some bills before rising from her chair.

He reached out to stop her. The second their hands touched, something changed in the air between them. Or maybe it was just him. He'd been trying so hard to push her away that now that she was leaving, he wanted her to stay. But when he looked up at her, he noticed subtle surprise playing out across her features, from the widening of her eyes to the parting of her lips.

She sank back into her chair, her attention never wavering from him.

And more important, she didn't try to pry his hand

away.

He wasn't ready to admit he needed her or anyone else, but somehow, confessing everything that had been bottled up inside for the last month eased the burden of guilt that had been weighing him down. Just knowing someone who'd been there was willing to listen and not call him weak or stupid or a lost cause made the darkness seem a little less impenetrable. And that gave him hope that he might succeed.

Yet his tongue refused to form the words to express his gratitude. Instead, what came out was, "I can pay."

The corners of her mouth rose into a smile that held no pity, no disappointment. If anything, she appeared to be proud of him. "You paid last week."

She slipped her hand out from under his and went to the counter to pay.

Ethan chugged the last of his coffee and tried to pull himself together. Maybe it was a good thing she was ending the night here. If she let him continue, who knew what else might come out of his mouth. As it was, he'd probably revealed too much about himself. It wouldn't take her long to put two and two together and figure out who he was.

And yet, oddly enough, he was okay with that. After all, she was Becca Shore. Even if she bore little resemblance to the person she'd been a few years ago, she probably still remembered how important privacy was when trying to stay clean.

He grabbed his helmet and followed her outside. A whiff of her perfume floated past him as she put her jacket back on against the cool autumn air. The scent evoked the memories of how well her body molded against his on the ride over, and a wayward twinge of desire stirred through his veins. "Can I give you a ride home?" he asked.

She bit her bottom lip, her pupils growing larger under the glow of the streetlights. Her gaze flickered to his motorcycle and then back to him. She inhaled, her body tightening up with excitement. Then her shoulders slumped as she released her breath. She took a step back and shook her head. "Thanks, but I'm going to have to pass. Besides, the subway's right over there."

Her rejection doused the heat in his blood. "I suppose I shouldn't have offered. The anonymous thing and all."

"No, it's not that." She gripped the shoulder strap of her bag, running her hands up and down it as she stared at the sidewalk. "As much as I'd like to, I know I shouldn't."

"Meaning?"

She looked up at him through her lashes long enough for him to see the attraction wasn't one sided. But she continued to back away. "I'll see you next week?"

His pride stung. She might have been turned on by him, but not enough for her to forget he was a recovering junkie. Thankfully, though, his wounded pride kept him from showing her how battered it really was. He stiffened his spine and got on his bike. "Maybe."

"Maybe?"

He refused to let her know how much of a sucker he had grown to be for her company. "Maybe."

Becca's lower lip jutted out into a pout that practically invited him to take it between his teeth. However, this wasn't some simpering trick meant to guilt trip him into saying yes. Based on the deepened furrow above her nose, this was actual bewilderment.

Good. Keep her guessing.

But when she turned around and started walking in the opposite direction, something shifted inside. His confidence fell like a trap door, plunging him into the pit of doubt. It dragged him under, surrounding him like quicksand and smothering the fragile hope he'd only recently discovered. His lungs burned for air, and his slick palms slipped off the throttle. She was leaving him alone with his inner demons. A black tunnel narrowed his vision, closing in on him.

He cried her name out in desperation.

She turned around, only few feet farther than she'd been. Not the miles his panic had imagined her to be. "Yes?" she asked, her voice rising with worry.

His heart rattled so hard a tremble shook his fingers, but the tightness in his chest eased enough to allow him to gulp in a breath of relief. She answered him when he called, just like she said she would. "Does it ever go away?"

He didn't need to elaborate. Her eyes darkened with regret. "No, but it gets easier with time."

"But there's no cure? No way to be completely free of it?"

She shook her head. "But remember what I said about filling the void with something else."

"And what if there *is* nothing else?"

Instead of fading in the distance, the click of her heels on the cement came closer. A set of fingers ran along his jaw and forced him to turn his head toward her. "Do you really believe that?"

The doubt grew louder, whispering in the back of his mind that he was nothing without his muse. "Do you?"

"No," she said in a hushed voice.

He longed to lift her hand to his cheek and press his head against her chest, soaking in all the comfort she could give him. But his pride wouldn't let him reveal how fucked up he was inside. He jerked his chin in the opposite direction and yanked on his helmet.

"Ethan, I meant what I said about calling me if you need to talk to someone. Don't give in to the doubt, the despair. It does get easier, and I'm here to help you in any way I can."

He revved up the engine and rode away before she discovered he was beyond help.

Chapter Four

Ethan placed his fingers on the familiar piano keys and willed them to create a melody. Growing up, he'd always found solace in music. Whenever he'd been frustrated with school or teased by his brothers, he could always sit in front of his mother's piano and release his angst through the dark and dreamy sonatas of Beethoven to the bright, bouncing beats of Gershwin. As he got older, he traded the classics for his own creations, expanding from the piano to his guitar. Whatever the song, he found peace through playing it.

But that was before music became a double-edged sword. Before playing what made him happy became what the record label would release. Before the pressure was laid on him to continue to write songs people would pay to hear. Before the thing that fed his soul only fed his bank account.

He banged his fist on the keys with a dissonant crash of notes and got up from the piano. It was eleven o'clock, a time when most normal people were getting ready to crawl into bed, but a nervous energy flowed through his blood, making sleep nearly impossible for the last three nights.

A Seductive Melody

The seed of doubt that had taken root as he left Becca the other night had bloomed into a dark jungle that threatened to swallow him whole.

He paced along the floor, the heel of his hand pressed against his temple. "Find something to fill the void. Find something to fill the void."

Once upon a time, that had been music, but now, that had been poisoned by heroin. He hadn't written any songs over the last three years without getting high. And no matter how hard he tried to go back to the way things had been, the craving proved stronger.

The only way to find peace was to give into his muse.

A snarl of frustration rolled up from the base of his throat, and he punched the brick wall. The pain in his hand dulled the ache in his heart. Now he understood why Ty could never give up his addiction, why his best friend never wanted to get clean and sober. When he was high, nothing mattered but the music, and the music calmed his soul. When he was high, he didn't hear the doubt. When he was high, he lived in a world of ignorant bliss, never knowing how close he actually was to losing it all.

"Find something to fill the void," he repeated.

He pulled Becca's number from the back of his wallet. His hand trembled as he stared at the numbers. All he had to do was call her, to hear her tell him he could get through this. His heart pounded as he imagined what he'd tell her. He was cracking up. Weak. A failure.

I'm not ready for that. I can get through this.

He crumpled the piece of paper into a ball and tossed it into the wastebasket filled with the shredded sheets of half-hearted compositions from the last three days.

If he couldn't play the music himself, then maybe he could find solace in listening to someone else play.

He grabbed his motorcycle and headed downstairs.

***

The Tin Lily hadn't changed much in the last past five years. It was the venue to play for rising rock groups, and the quivering in his gut as he walked through the front door reminded Ethan of the first time Ravinia's Rejects had been asked to take the stage. The East Village bar was loud and packed with a crowd that would either dance along with the music if it rocked or physically force the musicians off the stage if they sucked.

When he'd stepped up to the microphone that first time, he wasn't sure how the set would end for him and his friends, but Ty had given him a cocky grin and a wink before shredding the opening riffs of the song. Between the power of the music and the confidence Ty had instilled in him, he'd been able to open his mouth and give the performance of a lifetime. Two months later, that very song was sitting at the top of the rock charts, and Ravinia's Rejects was the band everyone was talking about.

Tonight, though, the vibe was much more subdued. A small group of dedicated rockers bobbed their heads up and down to the beat of the music, but the song played by the eighties cover band fell flat for him. He ordered a bottle of water at the bar and hoped the next song would be more inspiring.

But instead of getting lost in the music, he found himself picking it apart. A missed note. A wrong chord. A moment when the band was out of sync. And more than a dozen times when the lead singer was off pitch. No wonder they were just a cover band playing the late show on a Wednesday night.

He finished his water and was about to leave when a burly giant of a man blocked the path to the door. He cracked his knuckles in a way that dared Ethan to challenge him and said, "Someone wants to see you."

A slew of four-lettered words rolled through Ethan's mind as the moving mound of muscle led him up the balcony to a lone man leaning on the railing. A spotlight flashed on his face, and Ethan immediately drew to a stop.

Fuck!

If there was ever a time to avoid Ace, it was now.

The man came over to them, a big grin on his brown face. "Ethan Kelly, I thought that was you. I'd never forget that jacket of yours." Ace pulled him into a chest bump. "Long time no see, bro."

"Hi, Ace," he muttered out of mere politeness.

Ace's grin never faltered as he dismissed his henchman. "So, what brings you in tonight?"

In the past, that question would've been answered by asking what the dealer had on hand. Ace was a product of the hodgepodge of the Bronx—part black, part Dominican, and a mix of just about everything else. His global connections meant he had the best shit in Manhattan, and he'd grown rich supplying the rich and famous.

Ethan kept his attention fixed on the stage. "Just came to hear some music."

"Bad night for that, but you chose a good night to run into me. I just got a load of some awesome brown sugar."

Sweat prickled along the back of Ethan's neck. In the

past, he would've taken Ace up on his offer, taken it back to his hotel room, and let reality slip away for a few hours. But not tonight. He squeezed the railing to keep from giving into the craving. "Sorry, Ace, but I'm not into that anymore."

A look of shock slackened the dealer's features, followed by a nervous laugh. "Yeah, I heard about Ty. Sorry he's gone, man."

Yeah, I bet you're sorry. Ty had been one of his biggest clients.

"Then you understand why I'm no longer interested in your goods." Ethan pushed back from the railing.

"Hold on a minute, bro." Ace threw his arm around Ethan's shoulder and pulled him deeper into the balcony's shadows, his other hand in his pocket. "Let's talk about this."

A ripple of fear ran down Ethan's spine. Despite his friendly demeanor, Ace was not a man to be crossed. And if he was the least bit worried Ethan would rat on him, he wouldn't even bother with issuing a warning to be silent. He'd personally make sure Ethan wouldn't say a word to anyone.

But instead of pulling out a knife or a gun, he pulled out a tiny plastic bag with three glassine envelopes in it.

Ethan's pulse jumped. His brain warned him to leave now before he gave in to temptation, but he was mesmerized by the perfectly portioned hits of heroin.

"Listen, man, I don't normally do this, but you and Ty have been such good customers that this one can be on the house. And this ain't some crap, either. This shit is pure enough to sniff, but if you mainline it...." Ace rolled his eyes up to the ceiling and made a *mm-mm* sound more appropriate for a meal at a four-star restaurant. "Ah, it's absolute heaven."

His mouth watered. It sounded so simple, so easy to take Ace up on his offer and use it to get the music flowing again. One hit would be all he needed. One hit wouldn't put him in danger of an overdose.

But one hit would put him back to square one.

He buried his hands in his pockets to keep from touching it. "Ace, I—"

"You don't have to say anything, bro. I got you covered." Ace shoved the bag into Ethan's back pocket. "And when you need some more, you know how to reach me."

He wrestled free of the dealer and took a step back toward the stairs. "I won't need any more."

Ace laughed again, this time without the nervous vibe. It was hard and mocking. "Say that if it makes you feel better, but you and I both know you'll be back. Guys like you are nothing without the dope."

Ace waved him off, and Ethan ran down the stairs and out of the club as quickly as he could. The cool night air bathed the inside of his lungs with every breath he took. He stood in the middle of the sidewalk, letting the autumn rain wash away the contamination of the club.

This was his chance to throw away the bag Ace had stuffed into his pocket, but some part of his brain refused to let him. He had it if he absolutely needed it, but he wouldn't fall back on it. Not yet. He'd give himself a little more time to find the music before surrendering to his dangerous muse.

He rode home, threw the little bag on his coffee table, and stared at it from the sofa until the sky began to lighten.

***

Becca slipped into the empty seat next to Ari at Temple Israel. "Thanks for saving me a seat," she whispered.

"You're welcome." Ari nodded toward the man and woman seated five rows ahead of them. "Although it might be nice if you sit with your parents."

"Too late now," she replied as the rabbi called the congregation together for the start of Rosh Hashanah services.

Becca listened to the prayers and readings she'd grown up hearing every year for as long as she could remember, but this was the third year she'd chosen not to join her family in celebrating the Jewish New Year. Her heart cautioned her about the sin of pride, but there was a reason why she had to cut herself off from her parents. She wasn't strong enough yet to deal with the void they created inside her. As much as it hurt to avoid them, it was far better than falling back to her old ways of coping with their constant expectations of perfection.

During the silent *Amidah*, her thoughts wandered to Ethan. She hadn't heard from him, which was a good thing, but that still didn't keep her from worrying about him. Before he left Monday night, she could sense the rising desperation in him. Just hearing the pain in his voice when he described the loss of his best friend had her on the brink of tears, and it had taken every inch of willpower not to hold him in her arms and tell him everything would be okay. He was at the point where all recovering addicts were tested, and she offered her own prayer that reminding him of why he quit would be enough to keep him from relapsing.

A chill ran up her arms as she remembered the dark days of her own addiction. She glanced down at the veins in her arm and rubbed them, remembering all the times she'd celebrate finding one large enough to inject. Now they were scarred and shriveled up, a constant reminder of the damage she'd done to herself.

Becca turned her attention to her parents and caught her stepmother looking back at her. Her own mother had died from an overdose when Becca was still an infant, so Claire was the only mother she'd ever known. Her stepmother had spent the last two years trying to repair the gap between Becca and her father, but neither one of them yielded. Their gazes locked, and Becca caught a silent plea for forgiveness. It was so tempting to believe her father wanted to make amends, to make their family whole again. Claire turned away as the rabbi blew the shofar, leaving Becca to mull over the unspoken message. Maybe it would be nice to speak to her parents after services. Maybe they could go to the park afterward for the *Tashlich* and use it to cast away the pain of the past and begin again.

The idea grew on her as the service continued, but as she was kneeling during the closing prayers, the screen on her phone illuminated with a text message that chased away any thoughts of reconciling with her parents today.

Becca, it's Ethan. I really need someone to talk to. Now.

She discreetly pulled her phone out of her purse and checked the call log.

Eleven missed calls, all from the same number.

Shit!

She'd had her phone on silent for the prayer services so she wouldn't be disturbed, but now she risked losing the fragile trust Ethan had given her. She'd said she'd be there for him if he needed her, and she hoped God would understand if she exited Rosh Hashanah services early to help him.

She grabbed her purse and snuck out of the sanctuary, her head lowered until she was out on the street. Then she called him back. "Ethan, it's Becca."

"You said you'd answer." His voice was a growling mix of anger and panic.

She tried to combat it by adding layers of soothing tones to hers. "Yes, and I'm sorry I didn't answer. I had my phone on silent while I was at the Temple, and I shouldn't have done that. But I'm here now."

Silence hung on the line for nearly half a minute, and she prayed that Ethan would forgive her enough to tell her what was wrong.

"I need help," he said, his voice cracking.

"And I'm willing to do whatever I can to help. Just tell me what you need."

Another pause, followed by, "Oh, fuck it."

"No, don't say that." She wandered down the familiar sidewalks of 75th Street like a lost tourist, meandering from side to side and trying not to get run over. "Please, just tell me where you are, and I'll be there as quickly as I can."

A sarcastic snort of laughter answered her. "What about the whole anonymous thing?"

A Seductive Melody

Sure. Throw that back in my face when you need me. The only reason she'd declined a ride back to her place Monday night was because she feared she'd invite him upstairs and totally screw over their relationship by screwing him. "Fine, we can meet in a public place. How about Gitta's café?"

"Sorry, but I don't think sweets are going to help me. Face it, Becca, I'm fucked up, and there's no hope for me."

"Don't you dare say that, Ethan." Anger sharpened her words and made her wish he was standing next to her so she could smack some sense into him. "And don't you dare believe that, either."

"You don't know me, and you certainly don't know what I'm dealing with."

"Bullshit. I've been there—remember?" When he didn't reply right away, she remembered the plastic bag full of breadcrumbs in her pocket and formed a new plan. "What part of the city are you in right now?"

"Hell's Kitchen."

Of course he'd be there. It was one of the up-and-coming areas of Manhattan with several recording studios nearby. She did a mental check for places along the river where he could join her. "Can you meet me at the end of Pier 84?"

"Why?"

"Because it's public, and we can talk." She hailed a taxi. Traffic wasn't too bad right now, and the last thing she wanted to do was lose the connection to him while in the subway.

"Fine." He hung up on her just as a taxi pulled up to

the curb.

She gave the driver directions, her pulse fluttering in her ears the entire time.

Please let him be there.

And please don't let me be too late.

Chapter Five

Ethan stared into the Hudson River with a pair of sunglasses on, ignoring the people who milled around him. The rain from last night had dried up, but gray clouds still lingered overhead. They fit his mood.

Sometime after dawn, he'd managed to get a few hours of fitful sleep. He awoke tangled in sweat-soaked sheets, gasping for air and haunted by dark dreams. The craving was stronger than ever. It called to him like a siren's song that erased any rational thoughts. Not even a cold shower could quiet it.

The bag of heroin remained untouched on his coffee table, seducing him with promises to make everything better. But every time he found himself about to give into temptation, he glanced down at Ty's name on his arm. The memories of finding Ty dead assaulted him, growing stronger and stronger until he doubled over and let out a scream of frustration.

That was when he broke down, fished out Becca's number from the trash, and called her. It was better to admit he was weak than to end up like Ty.

But she didn't answer, and the world dropped out from

underneath him.

Now, an hour later, he was standing at the end of Pier 84, wondering if she would stand him up. He'd brought the bag with him. It mocked him from his back pocket while he waited. If she came, he'd ask her to dispose of it so he wouldn't be tempted any longer.

And if she didn't show…

He closed his eyes and wondered if taking a hit would ease his sense of abandonment. It would certainly cure his inability to play music. And maybe that would be the best course of action for now.

He spun around and collided with a woman, knocking her to the ground. It took him only a second to recognize her distinctive blue-green eyes. He knelt down to help her up. "Shit, Becca, I'm sorry."

"It's okay," she said, even though she winced as she limped to the railing. "I'd called out your name, but I guess you didn't hear me."

"Are you hurt?"

She shook her head. "My fault for running full speed toward you in high heels, but I was just so worried about you."

Something inside him did a one-eighty, and the insatiable craving that had plagued him for days retreated to the far corner of his mind.

She'd come.

She cared about him.

She was here to help him, and he wasn't alone.

And knowing that took him to a level of humble gratitude he'd never known.

"Thanks," he said softly.

"Of course." She turned her attention to the river. "So, what happened?"

He pulled the bag out of his pocket and showed it to her.

Horror, panic, and disbelief wash over her features. "Ethan, why?"

The disappointment in her voice rubbed his pride the wrong way and raised his hackles. "I haven't touched it."

"But you have it."

He tucked it back into his pocket. "Just wanted you to know why I called."

"So I could watch you get high again?"

"How do you know I wasn't inviting you to join me?" he snapped back, his words laced with sarcasm. "And before you say anything else, I didn't buy it. I didn't seek it out. It was given to me last night."

Her eyes narrowed, but he couldn't tell if her resentment was directed toward him or the person who'd given it to him. "By whom?"

"You wouldn't know him."

"Ace, right?"

His jaw fell slack. "How did you know?"

She gave a bitter laugh. "He always had the good stuff." She held onto the railing and rocked back on her heels. "Is he still hanging out at the Tin Lily on Wednesdays?"

If he'd ever doubted her past as an addict, her knowledge of Ace's hangouts confirmed it. "Yeah, he's still there. I'm surprised the cops haven't caught him, predictable as he is."

"That's because he has too many important people in

his pocket." She let go of the railing and ambled along the waterfront, Ethan following her. "That still doesn't explain what you were doing there last night."

"I went to listen to the music."

"Sure, and men read *Playboy* for the articles."

He darted in front of her, stopping her until she looked up at him. "No, really, I went for the music. And maybe to relive a few good memories."

She pursed her lips like she was trying to assess him on her bullshit-o-meter. "Take off your sunglasses," she ordered.

"Why?"

"Because I want to look into your eyes when you're answering me." When he complied, she asked, "Why did you go there last night?"

"To listen to the music," he repeated.

She came closer until her face was inches from his. Her hawk-like eyes picked him apart, looking for some sign of a lie, but all he could think about was how bright the green rings around the pupils were today.

She backed down. "You're going to have to start avoiding those kinds of places."

"Trust me—lesson learned." He moved aside so they could continue walking. "Ace caught me in a bad moment and said some things that pushed me to the edge."

"But not over it."

He paused and let her assessment sink in. He'd lost count of how many times he almost opened up that bag, but he hadn't. He'd been strong enough to resist. "Yeah, but not over it."

It still didn't change the fact he was caught in limbo as

far as his music went.

Becca looped her arm through his and resumed their stroll. "So you mentioned you were at a bad moment. Care to elaborate?"

"You wouldn't understand."

"Try me."

He looked down to where their arms entwined. And surprisingly, he liked it. He liked the weight of her arm against his. He liked the way her hips brushed against his thigh when she walked. He liked the subtle halo of her perfume that he inhaled every time the breeze caught it. But most important, he liked that she wasn't afraid to invade his personal space, and she didn't back down when he tried to push her away. If she'd been anyone else, he would've kept pushing. But walking arm in arm with her filled him with a momentary serenity he'd been missing for so many years.

"I'm a musician."

"I know," she replied as though he'd said he was something more commonplace, like a schoolteacher.

But did she know who he was? Did it even matter?

After a moment's hesitation, he decided not to bring his fame up. After all, she'd been famous—or infamous—herself. "I haven't been able to play since my best friend died."

"Can't play, as in you forgot how to strum a guitar?"

"No." Even though it wasn't far from the truth based on the clumsy way his fingers had been forming chords lately. He pulled his arm free and turned back to the railing. "I met my best friend at a music camp when I was twelve. He was a year older than me and represented so much of what I wanted to be. Fun. Outgoing. Crazy fucking talented. The guy could touch a guitar and spontaneously compose magic. So naturally, I looked up to him, and it wasn't long before we were best friends."

He stared into the murky water of the Hudson River, remembering all the fun they'd had as kids. "One thing led to another, and when he suggested we start a band with a couple of other guys in the neighborhood, I agreed. By the time we'd graduated from high school, we were already playing the local scene and decided to hit the road. Tin Lily was the venue that I always associated with making it to the big time. Once we played there, we became more than just some kids with a garage band. We were somebody."

"And is that what you meant by reliving some good memories?"

He nodded, but the burning along his left arm reminded him that those memories were now tainted. "But there was a dark side to our success. It didn't start out that way, you know? We were both just a couple of stupid teenagers who would light up a joint after practice. We weren't baked the entire time, but when we got high, that's when we wrote the songs that made us famous. And as our fame grew, so did the pressure to keep writing those kinds of songs.

"He started experimenting with the harder stuff first. A couple of Percocets here, a whiff of coke there. And like a dumbass, I tried whatever he offered me. The night we played Tin Lily was the first night I shot up."

He expected her to smack him on the back of his head like his mother did when he'd admitted to doing something stupid, but she stood next to him, mirroring his posture as she looked out over the river. "So you always associated getting high with the celebration of that night."

"Yeah. But later on that night, we composed our best song ever. Then one thing led to another, and before I knew what was happening, I discovered I couldn't write music without getting high first."

"Heroin became your muse," she said matter-of-factly, and a wave of relief flowed through him.

She understood him better than he thought she would.

"Yeah. But when it became my muse, it robbed me of the simple pleasures of playing. Now, every time I pick up a guitar or sit down at the piano, the craving consumes me."

"And I suppose asking you to stop being a musician is out of the question."

He tried to picture spending the rest of his life doing something different, but it would be like having the joy robbed from his soul. "No, I love music too much to quit playing."

"Then there's your answer."

"Maybe, but it still doesn't change the fact that I haven't been able to play since he died."

"Why?"

His stomach churned, and sweat coated his palms. She was treading on delicate ground here and digging up issues he wasn't ready to face yet. "I've already told you why."

She picked up on his unease and threw it back at him. Gone was the quiet listener from the other night. In her place stood a mirror reflecting the cold, hard truth. "No, you've told me that you were able to write music that got you to Tin Lily without ever touching heroin, and that you were a dumbass for trying whatever he offered you."

"That still doesn't change the fact that he's gone."

"He's gone because he was a selfish asshole who only thought of himself."

Her accusation touched a nerve in him, and he curled his fingers into his palms. How many times had he thought the exact same thing over the last month? And yet, he felt obligated to defend Ty. "Don't talk about my best friend like that."

"Some best friend. Let me guess—he was the one who gave you wings?"

His spine grew ramrod straight with annoyance. "Shut up, Bec."

But she didn't back down. Even though she never touched him, she stripped away his defenses. "Did you get sick to your stomach when he sank the needle into your vein? Did you cry like a baby from the head rush?"

His voice rose to a growl. "Shut. Up."

"Why did you do it, Ethan? Were you so desperate for his approval that you agreed to do anything he suggested? I bet he laughed his ass off when you were so high you couldn't even get up to take a piss."

Each question inched his anger level up a notch not because she was wrong, but because she was right. His temples throbbed with boiling rage that exploded with him shouting, "I said shut the fuck up."

As soon as he saw people around them staring at him, the blood rushed from his head, leaving a chill of fear behind. Jesus, he was cracking up. He staggered back a few steps before he turned around and headed back toward the city.

"Ethan, wait!" The click of her high heels on the pavers told him she was following him, but he refused to look back. "I'm sorry."

He drew to a stop and spun around, pointing his finger at her. "You have some nerve."

"Why? Because you're too chickenshit to hear the truth?"

His head started pounding again, this time from the storm of emotions raging inside. He squeezed his temples between his palms, willing it to stop, but the chaos grew stronger. Memories mixed with the craving and blurred his idea of reality until he felt like he was falling into a bottomless abyss.

"Let's sit down," a calm voice said over the noise in his head, followed by a gentle touch.

His feet stumbled in the direction she steered him, and he didn't resist when she guided him down to one of the nearby benches. The cool metal soothed him like ice on a bruise, but what finally brought some semblance of peace was the small hand that held his. The world came back into focus.

Becca squatted in front of him, worry tugging down the corners of her mouth. "Did I push you too far?"

"Yes," he said, his voice still raw from everything she'd unearthed.

"I only did it to help. I had to do something to erase the rosy glow you associated with getting high. I had to make you see the evil side of it, too. Until you come face to face with the truth, you can never move forward."

He stared at her hand in his, wondering how she could

touch him after learning so much about him. And yet the small gesture was a lifeline that was keeping him from drowning in his guilt and anger.

He filed through the past five years, taking each turning point and putting it in perspective. And when he reached the end, he said, "I wish I'd had the balls to tell him no."

She ran her thumb over the top of his hand, returning once again to the quiet listener.

He pulled up his sleeve to show her the tattoo with Ty's name. "I wish I'd said something sooner. Looking back, there were so many times I saw things getting out of control, and if I hadn't been so scared that I'd ruin our friendship and the band by speaking up…"

His eyes burned, and he blinked back the tears. She'd managed to rip him to the core, but he wasn't ready to cry in front of everyone on the pier. The emptiness gnawed at his chest. "There are just so many things I wish I'd done differently."

She nodded and cupped his cheek in her other hand.

This time, he allowed himself to savor the comfort she offered. He leaned forward until their foreheads touched. In and out, he matched her meditative breaths. Within a minute, his pulse had returned to normal, and the tension in his muscles unraveled. "Thanks, Bec."

"I'm not finished."

His gut clenched, and he pulled back. She'd already managed to send him to his private hell and brought him back. What more did she have in store?

Her grip held firm around his hand as she rose. "Come with me."

She led him back to the end of the pier, holding his

hand the entire time. When they reached the railing, she pulled out a plastic bag of breadcrumbs from her coat pocket. "Here, take some of these."

Confusion replaced his trepidation. "Are we going to feed the pigeons or something?"

"No, we're going to have our own little *Tashlich*." She poured some of the crumbs into his palm before grabbing a handful for herself. "It's a Rosh Hashanah tradition. Every year after morning services, we go to a river and sprinkle these crumbs into the water."

She demonstrated it to him with a pinch of the crumbs. "At the beginning of the new year, we cast off all our sins from the prior year. These crumbs are meant to represent all our faults, our shortcomings, our mistakes. And one by one, we rid ourselves of that burden while asking for forgiveness so we can start over and become better people."

She emptied out her palm and turned to him. "Now it's your turn. Let go of the anger, the guilt, the regret so you can move forward."

At first, he wanted to laugh and tell her that sprinkling bread crumbs into the Hudson wouldn't cure him of the emptiness inside, but with every pinch, his mood lightened. He couldn't change the past. He couldn't correct his mistakes. And he couldn't bring Ty back.

But he could move forward.

His palm was empty before he realized it. "Got some more?"

"Absolutely." She handed over the bag.

"Good, because I have a whole lot of shit to get off my back." He tipped the bag over and shook it until the very last crumb fell into the water. Then he watched them flow away while holding her hand.

"Feeling better?" she asked.

He rubbed his chest, noting how the hollowness inside seemed smaller than before. "Yeah."

"Good." She stepped back from the railing. "Ready to go?"

He nodded, but there was one more thing he needed to do. He reached into his back pocket and pulled out the bag of heroin Ace had given him last night. "I don't need this anymore."

He hurled it out into the Hudson. The breeze caught it and whipped it into a few dizzying circles before it hit the water and finally sank beneath the waves.

"If we hear reports of a massive number of fish washing up on shore, we know who to blame," she teased, but the admiration in her eyes replaced the emptiness he'd harbored inside with a warm glow.

He wanted her to always look at him that way. He wanted to be a man she could be proud of.

She took his hand again as though they were on a date rather than a crisis intervention. "So, do you have any plans for the evening?"

"No, not really."

"Want to come over to my place?" The blood rushed to his dick at her invitation, but his desire was quickly tempered when she continued, "My roommate and I are having a Rosh Hashanah party with our friends."

As tempting as it sounded, something in him hesitated. She was willing to tear down the shield of anonymity by bringing him into her personal life, and that opened the door to all types of possibilities, both good and bad. "I'm not Jewish."

"We'll let that one slide."

"Listen, Bec, I appreciate the invitation, but—"

She stopped and turned to him. "But what?"

Indecision paralyzed his tongue. He enjoyed Becca's company. Probably more than he should, considering relationships were discouraged this early in the recovery process. And the attraction was undeniable. But if he took things too far, presumed too much, he risked losing her support. And he didn't even want to think about what would happen if one of the guests recognized him.

He rubbed the back of his head. "I—"

"It's just my friends, Ethan. We're going to dance, play a few games, eat some food, and have a good time. No pressure." She lowered her voice and added, "And no worries. They respect my privacy, and they'll respect yours."

Suspicion snaked down his spine. It wasn't the first time she'd hinted that she knew who he was. "So I won't have to worry about ending up on TMZ?"

She grinned and shook her head. "Now, of course, what happens when you leave my place is a different story, but my friends are cool."

He almost wanted to laugh at how normal it sounded. He couldn't remember the last time he'd hung out with regular people his own age. "Maybe just for an hour or two."

"Brilliant!" She looped her arm through his, pressing up against him. "Did you bring your bike?"

"Yes."

"Any chance you'd let me drive it?"

He let out an honest, heartfelt laugh. "Nope."

"Didn't think so." She gave him a dramatic sigh. "I guess I'll have to ride bitch again."

He liked the idea of her riding behind him. Maybe he would even throw in some extra speed around the turns so she'd gasp and hold on even tighter to him. He handed her his spare helmet when they got to his motorcycle. "Where to?"

"Park and 75th."

"Upscale neighborhood." He donned his gloves and started the engine.

"Of course. Old money and all that." She climbed on behind him, her dress rising to expose most of her thighs.

His pants grew uncomfortably tight. Maybe he wouldn't go so fast around those turns if he wanted to be able to walk without an obvious hard-on when they got there.

Just as he was about to strap on his helmet, she tapped his shoulder. "Oh, by the way, we need to stop and pick up some challah."

"Yes, ma'am."

As they rode through the streets, he reflected on all the new emotions he was experiencing. Trust. Relief. Desire. Hope. So very different than when he'd arrived at the pier an hour before. And he owed it all to Becca.

But as they got closer to her place, a new goal replaced just staying clean. He was making a fresh start, and if he was lucky, maybe she'd begin to see him as something other than a recovering junkie who needed her help.

Maybe she'd begin to see him as a man worthy of her

A Seductive Melody

attention.

Chapter Six

Becca hopped off Ethan's bike and shivered. The ride had left her bare legs cold and numb, but the excitement of holding him as he expertly weaved his way through the traffic more than made up for it. "That was awesome!"

He turned off the engine and removed his helmet. "If you like my Ducati so much, why don't you just buy one?"

"Um, it's not that simple." She didn't want to explain that when she'd cut her parents out of her life, they'd cut her off financially. Sure, she had a trust fund, but she didn't have access to it until she was twenty-five, thanks in part to her history of addiction. That meant any future Ducati purchases were on hold for another two years.

"I'll be happy to give you a ride whenever you'd like, then."

A flush of heat rose up her neck into her cheeks. After all the crap she put him through, he was still being generous with her. It had been a dangerous move to switch tactics on him, to turn his pity party into a finger-pointing session. He could've told her to fuck off and walked away. But when he'd shown her those packets of heroin, she knew drastic measures were needed.

She offered a small prayer of thanks that it had worked.

And the change was remarkable, even after such a short time. The light had returned to his gray eyes, and his mouth curved more readily into a smile than a scowl. In fact, he was downright sexy.

Cool your jets, Becca. You just brought him back from the brink of disaster. Wait until he's stable before making a move on him.

She pulled the doughnut she'd picked up at the bakery out of her purse and gave it to the doorman. "*Shanah Tovah*, Stan."

"And Happy New Year to you, Miss Rebecca." He held the door open for her and Ethan. "Miss Ariella already has a few guests."

"Which means I'm a bit late." She pushed the up button for the elevator. "I'll probably get dragged to the kitchen as soon as we get up there."

Ethan's expression remained unreadable, but the line of his shoulders stiffened. "Can I do anything to help?"

"Maybe. But if you just want to hang out, you can do that, too."

A flicker of unease flashed in his eyes just before the elevator doors opened.

They got inside, and she looked up at him. "If you're not ready for this—"

"No, I want to do this." He gave her a wry smile. "Correction: I need to do this. I've been hiding under my shell too much lately."

She gave his hand a small squeeze. "My friends are fun. You'll see."

But a small part of her hoped none of them would figure out who Ethan was and make a big deal about it.

After all, they'd hung out with her and Ari's brother, Gabe, who was a celebrity in his own right. Bringing a rock star to one of their groups shouldn't cause that much of an uproar.

The aromas of pomegranate glazed chicken and blackberry BBQ beef brisket greeted her when she opened the door. Aaron and Levi had already hooked up the Xbox and were so involved with their first person shooter game that they didn't even turn around. Ari, however, rounded the corner from the kitchen and stopped short when she saw Ethan. "Who's this?"

"Ethan." No need to explain any further.

Ari's jaw tightened, and she grabbed Becca's arm in a death grip to drag her back into the kitchen. "Is this that junkie?" she whispered.

"He's clean, Ari, and I didn't want him to be alone tonight."

"But he's not one of us."

"So?" She peered into the living room. Aaron and Levi had paused their game long enough to start chatting with him, pointing to his helmet and probably asking about his motorcycle. A few exchanges later, Ethan had shed his jacket and was pushing up the sleeves of his gray thermal shirt, preparing to join them in the game. "He seems to be fitting in with the guys just fine."

"That's because they don't know what he is."

Becca took a deep breath to keep from telling Ari who he really was. It was one thing if Ethan had revealed his identity to her, but he hadn't. And until he did, she would respect his privacy.

"I can vouch for him, Ari. He's a good guy."

Her roommate's brown eyes darkened. "Fine, but if he steals any of our stuff to buy drugs, I'm holding you responsible."

The doorbell rang, and Ari went to answer it.

Becca pressed her forehead against the cold stainless steel of the fridge. She hadn't expected Ari to be such a snob. At least Aaron and Levi seemed open to letting Ethan join their party.

Female voices filtered into the kitchen, and Becca took another peek into the living room. Morgan and Natalie had arrived. Gabe had always jokingly referred to Ari, Nat, and Morgan as the Bimbo Barbie Brigade, but the description fit. They were all sleek, tanned, blond, and elegant, but superficial at times. Her stomach sank as Natalie made her way over to Ethan and started flirting with him.

Of course she would. He was good-looking. And charming. And had this sexy charisma about him. What woman wouldn't be attracted to him?

But he smiled and then jerked his head in Becca's direction. Natalie's seductive smile fell into a pout, but Becca's grin widened. He'd just made it very clear he was with her, and her heart skipped a few beats.

She opened the fridge and grabbed the tray of sliced apples she'd prepared first thing that morning. A small bowl of honey went in the center before she carried it out into the room. "Who's ready for the first course?"

The guys paused their game, and everyone gathered around her to grab an apple slice and dip it in the honey. Ethan was the last one to take a slice. He watched the others before following their example. "It's good," he said after the first bite. "I'd always wondered why you serve apples and honey, though."

Morgan backed away, her perfect nose wrinkling. "You're a *shegetz*?"

"Um, maybe?" He turned to Becca for assistance.

"He's not Jewish," she told the others, "but he's still cool."

"Hey, no one's perfect," Levi replied between stuffing more apple slices in his mouth. "Well, except for me."

The group broke out in chuckles and snickers, and Aaron gave Levi a playful shove. Levi's narcissism was a common joke among them, but it took the focus off Ethan. They all broke away, leaving him with her.

He closed the space between them, his voice dropping to a low, gravelly tone that oozed sex. "So I'm cool, huh?"

"Yeah, even though you have a dribble of honey on your chin." She grabbed it with her finger and wiped it up.

He caught her hand and brought her finger to his lips, removing the honey with a slow, sensual suck that left the place between her legs wet with want. "Pretty sweet stuff."

If he kept talking to her like that, she'd be dragging him to her bed before the next course was served. *Keep it together, Becca. Focus on something other than how much he's turning you on.* "That's the whole idea behind Rosh Hashanah dinner. A sweet new year."

"I can live with that." He continued to stare at her like he wanted to remove honey from other parts of her body until Aaron called him back to the game.

Becca retreated to the kitchen, every inch of her skin flushed with arousal. If she'd had any doubts about taking things to the next level, Ethan had just erased them. But she had to take things slowly or she risked having all this blow up in her face.

Take your time, Becca. You don't want a quick fuck to jeopardize the trust you've built so far.

But one thing was certain. Ethan Kelly knew how to push her buttons in all the right ways.

Chapter Seven

As much as Ethan tried to focus on the game he was playing with Levi and Aaron, the sweet taste of Becca's finger in his mouth kept ambushing him. Now that was a craving he could easily become addicted to. He'd love to sample other parts of her, starting with her lips. And then, if he worked up his courage, he could invite her back to his place for the main course.

But the moment he thought about her in his bed, his palms grew damp. He couldn't remember the last time he'd made love to a woman sober. Hell, he'd lost his virginity while drunk and stoned at a party. Years of being on the road didn't leave much time for a long-term relationship, and one-night flings had become his norm. After a few beers or a quick shot of H, he no longer cared that he didn't have someone special to come home to. He had a warm body for the night, and that was all that had mattered.

Until now.

He was twenty-five. Not quite ready to settle down, but ready to actually give a serious relationship a try. And Becca was a girl worth taking that risk for.

Now, to get over the performance anxiety issues.

One of the blondes—Natalie, he thought—handed him a bottle of hard apple cider. He set it aside, untouched, and continued playing until the front door opened, and a guy shouted, "*Shanah Tovah*, bitches!"

Levi and Aaron threw down their controllers and went to greet the new arrivals. Four more guys and three more girls poured into the apartment, and the atmosphere changed from a few friends hanging out to a full-on party. Voices filled the room, vying with the ever louder music that pumped in from the built-in surround-sound speakers. Becca's roommate circled the room with a tray of appletinis, and Becca appeared from the kitchen with a platter of steaming chicken.

"Time for the next course," she announced over everyone. "Pomegranate chicken."

Ethan's mouth watered from the sweet and savory aromas that filled the apartment. He got in line behind the others for a slice of the roasted chicken covered with a tangy red sauce and chunks of fresh pomegranate. "You made this?" he asked.

Becca nodded. "Amazing what an electric roaster can do."

He ate a bite. It tasted even better than it smelled. "Is this another tradition?"

"Yes. The pomegranate symbolizes a new year full of good deeds." She looked out at her guests, who were busy chatting and drinking with their friends. "Although I wished we could've done the Kiddush before they dived in."

"This is our party, not our parents'," her roommate

said, grabbing another slice of chicken. "We don't have to do all the stuffy traditional stuff. If you wanted that, then you should've had dinner with your family."

Becca blinked hard and turned away, but not before he caught a glimpse of pain on her face. Something her roommate said had hurt her, and he found himself reaching to comfort her before he could stop himself.

"You okay?" he asked.

"Yeah." She flashed a half-hearted smile to him. "You?"

He glanced around the room and nodded. "Yeah, I am, actually."

"Good." Her smile warmed, and she handed him a bottle of water. "I need to get back to the kitchen to start the next course."

"I'll be here."

A moment later, Levi was dragging him back into the group and introducing him to the new arrivals. Ethan stood on the fringes, listening and only speaking when asked a question. He nursed his bottle of water instead of guzzling hard cider down like the other guys. And even though his reclusive inner nature recoiled at the idea of a party full of strangers, he found himself warming up to Becca's friends as quickly as he had to her.

A knock could barely be heard over the noise, but Becca went to answer it. A man carrying two guitars—one strapped to his back and the other in his hand—entered the party and gave her a hug.

The jealousy that flared within Ethan's gut as they talked surprised him. What if this was her boyfriend? What if he was falling for a girl who was already with someone?

A Seductive Melody

Was that why Becca had been hiding out in the kitchen all night? He crossed the room to learn more about the latest guest.

The man was removing the electric guitar strapped to his back when he got there. "Who's this, Becca?" he asked, eyeing Ethan as more of a curiosity than competition.

"This is my friend Ethan."

Friend. The word stung harder than a slap in the face. He should be grateful she considered him a friend, but now he wanted more.

The man held out his hand. "Hi, Ethan. I'm David."

He took his time accepting the hand, the unease pounding through his veins as he studied the latest arrival. David was dressed in a nice button-down shirt and khakis and had a full beard that made his age difficult to guess.

Becca stood with one hand placed on each man's shoulders, gauging their reactions to each other with a hopeful grin. "David's a musician, too, Ethan. He's finishing up his cantorial studies at the HUC."

Nice to know, but it still didn't answer the one question that jabbed the corners of his mind like a pissed-off hornet.

"Becca," Ari called from the kitchen, "the brisket."

Her face paled. "Oh, no." She dashed off, leaving him alone with the man who might be her boyfriend.

"So, Ethan, what do you play?"

He was trying to make small talk, but Ethan couldn't relax. "Guitar, mostly. But I also play piano, drums, trumpet."

"Nice. Have you ever thought about playing for the

Temple?"

"He can't," Morgan answered for him, slipping her arm through David's. "He's a *shegetz*."

David's smile widened. "Any chance of converting?"

"Not likely."

"Too bad," David replied, ignoring Morgan's attempts to pull him away from the door. "We could use some more musicians."

The blonde interrupted with a huff and roll of her eyes. "Can't this wait?"

He soothed her with a kiss on the cheek. "Give me a minute, hon."

The tightness in Ethan's forearms eased. From the looks of things, David had his hands full with Morgan.

"But you've been gone all day with that thing at the Temple." She gave him the spoiled rich girl simper.

"Yes, and I'll be with you in just a minute. I haven't even taken my coat off."

Morgan's pout deepened, but she backed away holding up a single finger. "One minute."

"Sorry about that," David said with a sheepish shrug as he slipped off his coat. "She's upset because I'd promised to play for the afternoon services and couldn't be here when the party started."

"Is that why you have two guitars?" Ethan leaned to the side to get a better look at the cases, recognizing the brands. Fender. Martin. Signs of a serious musician.

"Yeah." He hung up his coat in the closet. "Maybe we can jam later. I have an app that turns my phone into an amp."

An icy blast of fear paralyzed him. It was one thing to

not be able to play when he was alone, but to freeze up in front of Becca's friends was an entirely different matter. He wasn't ready to make a fool of himself just yet. "Maybe," he said in a tight voice.

He was saved by Levi shouting, "Becca's bringing out the brisket."

The party guests gathered around the dining room table, where Becca carved up the medium rare slab of beef into thin slices. The outside was covered by a blackened glaze, and a small bowl held what looked like a dark barbecue sauce. Ari added a salad made with baby greens, pomegranate seeds, and apples. The other women poured out of the kitchen with the rest of the sides such as mashed sweet potatoes, candied carrots, round loaves of challah, and green peas. Once everything was set, they loaded up their plates.

As Ethan tasted the dishes, he noted the sweetness of each one and inwardly grinned. Becca's sweet tooth would be in heaven tonight. Even the salad was tossed in a honey vinaigrette.

After she'd filled her plate, Becca gestured for him to meet her at the dining bar that looked into the kitchen. "Like it so far?"

"Best food I've eaten since I came into town." And he meant that. The takeout he'd been living on was sawdust compared to a home-cooked meal. Once again, her generosity had humbled him. "Thank you for inviting me."

"I told you my friends were cool." She gave him a wink and popped a sliced carrot into her mouth. "By the way, I hope you don't mind me telling David you're a musician."

"No, not really." He was more upset about being introduced as a friend, despite his head telling him "friend" was good enough considering how long they'd known each other.

"I figured since he was a musician, too, he might be able to help you find the music again."

"Doubt it." But her suggestion hovered around him like a swarm of gnats for the rest of the meal, never giving him a moment's peace until he was forced to get up and go out on the balcony to clear his head.

The crisp autumn air cooled his frustration. The setting sun bathed Central Park and the rest of the city in an orange glow. From this height, everything appeared calm and serene, and his soul followed suit. The balcony was more of a large patio that ran the length of the apartment, wide enough to allow two lounge chairs and a bistro set. It would be perfect for summer barbecues, but right now, the openness contrasted with the crowded confines inside. Here, he could see the sky and collect himself.

He didn't bother turning around when he heard the door open behind him. Becca was the only one who'd dare come out there to join him.

But it was a male voice that said, "Care to have that jam session now?"

Ethan turned around to find David sliding two chairs together next to a pair of acoustic guitars. "What about the rest of the party?"

"It's too loud in there. Besides, if we start playing, they'll join us." He opened one of the cases. "Do you prefer the Martin or the Taylor?"

"Doesn't matter." He doubted his fingers would

remember the chords.

"You can use Ari's." David handed him the practically new Taylor and opened the hard case of the Martin. "Or, if you prefer, I can give up my Martin for a bit."

"It's really not necessary." He tried to hand the guitar back, but David refused to take it. "I haven't been much in the mood for playing lately anyway."

"That's a pity. Music always soothes me." He strummed the strings and closed his eyes.

Ethan recognized the beginning chords of the Beatles song. His fingers wrapped around the neck of the guitar in his hand, moving in time to the transitions, but it took a gulp of courage to run the pick over the strings and join in. David's clear baritone filled the night with a sharpness that cut away the guilt and doubt imprisoning Ethan's soul. The chains binding his music broke, leaving behind the weightless joy he remembered from his youth.

By the time David got to the chorus, Ethan joined in. The resulting harmony surprised him. He'd been the lead singer for so long, he'd forgotten what it was like to play backup, and yet the hard edge of his voice mingled perfectly with David's classically trained one. The unadorned quality reminded him he still had a decent voice, and the impromptu jam session was miles away from the glare of the center stage spotlight. Maybe he could make music without Ty, without drugs, without the complex sound engineering provided by the studio.

Becca's friend gave him an encouraging smile before launching into the next verse. When the chorus rolled around again, his confidence grew, and he carried over the harmony from his voice to his guitar. The challenge was fun and refreshing, and the corners of his mouth started to rise.

He'd rediscovered his love for music.

"You sure you won't consider converting?" David said as they finished. "I'd love to have you in the Temple band."

"Thanks, but I just got out of a band, and I'm taking a little time off for me." He strummed the strings once and resisted the urge to hug the borrowed guitar. "You up for another?"

"Absolutely. You pick."

Ethan searched his mind for a song that wasn't a Ravinia's Rejects tune and went with another classic Extreme song perfect for two voices and acoustic guitars. He set his pick aside and used his fingers to form the opening chords.

"Good one." David played along, but when it came time for the words, he nodded and said, "This one's all yours."

It's just Becca's friend on a balcony, not a crowded stadium. You can do this.

The first few notes warbled with a gravelly tone, a result of weeks of inactivity, but he recovered by the second line and lost himself in the music. It wasn't until they reached the end that he realized they'd gathered an audience.

Heat rose up his neck to the tips of his ears. All this time, he'd been trying to lay low, and now he might have lost his anonymity by opening his mouth. He searched the crowd who'd gathered around, looking to see if any of them recognized him. But the second he saw Becca's beaming face, all thoughts about protecting his privacy vanished. She seemed so proud of him, he didn't care what the others thought. Only her opinion mattered.

"That was awesome," the guy who'd made the loud entrance said, holding up a lighter. "Keep it comin', bros."

"Can we move it inside?" Morgan asked as she rubbed her bare arms. "It's a little chilly out here."

"No problem." David rose, carrying his guitar, but Ethan remained in his seat.

Less than twenty-four hours ago, he'd been ready to relapse, to surrender to heroin just so he could find the solace it gave him. But all this time, the music was right there for him to grasp. He just had to shed the trappings he'd secured around it and recover the essential core.

I can really do this. I can still play and stay clean.

Now the challenge would be to create new music without relying on his former muse.

"Are you coming, Ethan?" Becca asked softly.

He turned to find her standing beside him with her hand held out.

He took it and stood up, finding the strength to keep moving forward because of her support. "Yeah, I am."

She leaned in and whispered, "I'm glad you found the music again."

If he didn't have an audience on the other side of the glass doors, he would've pulled her into a kiss right then. Instead, he settled for tucking a strand of her dark hair behind her ear. "Me, too."

Once inside, he and David took turns playing classic rock songs for the group and entertaining a few of their requests. It was fun until Ari called out one of his band's songs. Ethan drew in a deep breath and held it. If he catered to the request, he once again risked blowing his cover.

"I don't know that one very well," David said. "Do you know it, Ethan?"

He nodded, not trusting his own voice. He searched for Becca, but couldn't find her. Fear wormed along his gut.

I have to do this alone.

But as his gaze swept the room and he saw David's encouraging nod, it dawned on him that he wasn't alone. He strummed the opening chords from memory. The acoustic guitar was softer, slower than the electric guitar he was used to playing for that song, but it allowed him to do the same with the lyrics. A rasp of emotion filled his voice as he sang the opening verse of the song. It was the first Ravinia's Rejects song he'd sung since Ty had died, and the solemn quality it took on with the acoustic guitars fit his mood. It was a eulogy of sorts, a way for him to say good-bye to the past.

David joined in, but the sound wasn't the same as when Ty had played harmony. It was different, but in a good way. As the song drew to a close, his fingers itched to play new music, to twist and shape the chords into an expression of conflict raging inside him.

"Whoa," Ari said, her eyes wide. "That was even better than the original."

It had better be, considering I was the one who wrote it.

"Thanks," he mumbled and rose from his chair. He needed to find Becca. "Time for a little break."

"Same here." David set his guitar aside and pulled

Morgan into his arms.

The loud techno music from earlier blasted through the speakers just as Becca appeared from behind a closed door with a stack of paper. She beckoned him over, and he came, still clutching her roommate's guitar.

"I heard the new arrangement, and it got me to thinking. Maybe you should make some notes." She held out a stack of blank sheet music. "I printed these off for you, but if you need more…"

The woman could read him better than he did himself. He took the stack and placed a chaste kiss on her forehead. "Do you have a quiet place I could hang out in?"

"You can use my bedroom." She opened the door she'd just come out of.

"Thanks." He held her gaze for a moment to make sure she knew the full extent of his gratitude. She'd helped him overcome a major hurdle to his recovery, and he finally felt like he was moving forward.

Her eyes sparkled with excitement. "You're welcome."

Becca's room was simple and serene, much like her. The blue colors and clean lines quieted his anxiety and sharpened his focus. He sat down on the edge of the bed with Ari's guitar and jotted down the notes for the new arrangement. His pen halted when he read the line she'd written at the top of each page.

Words and music by Ethan Kelly.

It confirmed that she knew who he was, and yet she treated him as she did the rest of her friends. She didn't kiss his ass or handle him with kid gloves. He was just another person to her, and that made him trust her all the more with his secrets.

He finished his notes and pulled out a blank sheet. It was time to create something new.

Chapter Eight

The party had taken a drunken turn for the worse by the time Ethan emerged from Becca's bedroom. Slurred words battled over the pulsating music, and arms and legs flopped around in staggering dance moves.

Ethan made his way around the edge of the living room, looking for Becca and bumping into her roommate instead. She looked up at him with glazed brown eyes and made no effort to untangle herself from him. "You have a sexy voice," she drawled.

"Where's Becca?" His words were sharp and forceful, a direct contrast to her languid, liquor-laden one. There was only one woman he wanted pressed up against him, and it wasn't the petite blonde.

She backed off with a slight pout. "Out on the balcony."

As before, the wide balcony offered a respite from the chaos inside. He scanned the dimly lit area, starting with the chairs and finally finding her leaning against the wall in a far corner. "Hey," he said as he came toward her, giving her plenty of time to say she wanted to be alone if needed.

"Hey," she replied. "How did it go?"

"Good." He stopped in front of her and braced his elbow against the warm bricks. "Really good, actually. I wrote a new song."

"Care to sing a few bars for me?"

A self-deprecating laugh broke free from his chest. "Still working on the lyrics."

"They'll come to you." She sighed and looked up at the sky. "Sorry for hiding out on you, but I needed to get away from that environment before I did something I'd regret."

He leaned in closer, inhaling her perfume. His dick stiffened, and all thoughts of music vanished. "Meaning?"

"I don't drink because it's too risky for me. But the rest of them...." She shrugged as though the way the party had eroded explained itself.

"So that was the mistake you were worried about making?" He came close enough to hear her breath catch.

She looked up at him, her eyes darkening with desire. She licked her lips. "Among other things."

He kept closing in, waiting to see if she would push him away. The next thing he knew, his lips were brushing against hers in a hesitant, feather-light kiss. Warmth flooded his insides from the point of contact, and yet fear tempered his desire. He pulled back a few inches to gauge her reaction.

Her eyes were closed, but a blissful smile gave him permission to continue.

This time, he made his kiss more forceful, more demanding. He wanted to push the boundaries of their relationship and see how far she was comfortable going. She yielded to him and parted her lips. He greedily explored the sweetness of her mouth while his fingers still dug into the grout between the bricks. She tasted so good that if he dared to take her into his arms, he wouldn't be satisfied until he had her in bed.

The slow, sensual kiss seemed go on forever. He never imagined he'd enjoy the simple pleasure of kissing a woman like this, but kissing Becca was far better than the years of hazy hookups he'd experienced. He zeroed in on all her subtle responses, acutely aware of how she responded to him. Her breath quickened, and she reached to touch him. First, it was his chest. Then, his shoulders. Finally, her hands wound around his neck while she deepened the kiss. The last traces of his uncertainty melted. She wanted him as much as he wanted her, and he allowed himself to thread his fingers through her silky hair.

"Becca," Ari called from the door.

Ethan tore his lips from hers and jumped back. As much as he wanted to continue, he didn't want the intimate moment to become a spectacle.

"What?" Becca replied, making no attempt to hide the exasperation in her voice.

"We're going to Cielo. Want to come with us?"

Becca looked up at him, her pupils wide and her chest still rising and falling rapidly. "I think I'll stay in tonight."

"I thought you'd say that."

She grinned and turned toward her roommate. "Be safe."

"You, too." Ari gave him a hard glare before shutting the door.

He waited for her to say anything, but when the silence crept on, he said, "I don't think she likes me."

"She's just being the overprotective best friend. If she

knew who you were, she'd act differently."

"Meaning?" He waited for her to say what he already knew.

Her cheeks flushed, and she looked away. "I think Ari's an even bigger Ravinia's Rejects fan than I am."

"And you didn't tell her."

Becca shook her head. "To be honest, it took me a week or two to figure it out myself. But if you're willing to go to such extreme measures to hide who you are, the least I can do is keep my mouth shut."

He ran his thumb over her bottom lip. "Such a tempting mouth, too."

Even the dim light couldn't conceal the blush that bloomed in her cheeks. "A simple thank-you would be fine."

His shoulder blades drew together, and he added some distance between them. "Are you telling me I went too far?"

"No, I—" She grabbed his shirt in her fists and pulled him back into another kiss. This time, she called the shots, controlling the tempo like a maestro conducting an orchestra. It started out with a smooth, slow adagio pace and grew into a lively allegro.

Her passion infiltrated him and tore down the restraints holding his desire in check. He pressed her against the wall, one hand still tangled in her hair while the other cupped the curve of her ass. Every seductive kiss, every flick of her tongue, every delicious moan that rose from her throat made his cock harder. His hips rocked back in forth in the grinding dance he wanted to replicate under the covers.

A Seductive Melody

He wanted her so damned badly.

But he wasn't prepared to respond when she ended the kiss and asked, "Do you want to take this to my bedroom?"

***

Holy shit! What just came out of my mouth?

Becca hadn't intended to proposition Ethan tonight, but each kiss continued to whittle away at her common sense until she was so horny, the question slipped out before she had a chance to catch herself.

He stiffened and retreated a few inches, his brows drawing closer together. "Becca, I…"

Her heart sank as he squeezed his eyes shut and took a step back.

Pride kicked in, and she fumbled for words to hide her embarrassment. "Sorry, I just—"

He silenced her by tilting her chin up so she was forced to look him directly in the eyes. "Don't be."

"No, I crossed the line, and I've obviously made you uncomfortable and—damn it!" She dug her fingers into her palms and turned toward the door. She shouldn't have asked him. It was still too early in the recovery process for him to jump into a sexual relationship. And yet he'd made such huge strides today, she'd almost forgotten where he'd been that morning. "I knew I'd fuck this up somehow."

Ethan caught her wrist and spun her back against him. "Do I look like I'm uncomfortable?"

A rock-hard ridge strained against his zipper and pressed against her lower stomach. "I don't know. You tell me."

"I think it's quite obvious how turned on I am right

now." He gave her a quick kiss, drawing out the end by sucking on her bottom lip. "I know you're trying to look out for me, and I appreciate that. If you tell me to stop, I will, but if you want to continue…"

The little voice inside her head told her to stop things now, but the desire proved too much. "I do."

She grabbed his hand and led him inside. Ari and the rest of their friends had already left for the club. The place was wrecked, but she'd deal with that in the morning. Right now, all she cared about was getting Ethan in her bedroom before she lost her nerve.

As soon as the door shut, she pulled him to her again. Their kisses took on a frantic nature as though they were two teenagers who wanted to come before they got caught by their parents. She tugged his shirt off, taking a second to admire the tattoos covering his lean frame before diving into the next breathless kiss.

Ethan fumbled for the zipper of her dress, but when it hit a snag, he broke off the kiss with a growl of frustration. "Turn around."

A shiver coursed down her spine. In everyday life, she hated men ordering her around. But in the bedroom, it was a different story.

He finally got her dress off, followed by her bra, leaving her to stand in the chilly bedroom with her back to him. He drew back her hair to expose the nape of her neck and pressed his lips against the skin. "How do you like it?"

Her stomach fluttered. Would he be put off by her submissive preferences? "You tell me."

He chuckled and wrapped his arms around her chest to

cup her breasts in his hands. "Are you going to make me guess?"

"No." She leaned back against him, savoring the heat of his bare chest. "You tell me."

He froze as her request sank in. Then he tightened his hold on her and tilted her to the side so his warm breath bathed her ear. "I tend to get a little rough."

To prove his point, he squeezed her nipples as he caught her earlobe between his teeth. The sharpness of the pain made her breath catch and sent a bolt of desire straight to her sex. He followed the brief sting with soothing flicks of his tongue and a gentle massage of her breasts. Just as she was forgetting the rough play, he repeated the action with the same effect on her.

He gave another low chuckle as though he knew exactly how much his teasing was turning her on. "Tell me if it's too much."

The next few minutes were a tango of pleasure and pain. For every nip or pinch, he'd take his time soothing the injured flesh, lulling her back into a relaxed state before jolting her arousal again. His mouth explored the back of her neck, her shoulders, her arms, while his hands stayed on her breasts. His erection pressed against her ass the whole time, a constant reminder of what lay in store for her.

The pleasure–pain cycle became faster, more intense, until he finally released her. His voice was raw and panting as he said, "Turn around and take off your panties."

She complied with the first part of his order and met his gaze. The fiery desire in his eyes and rapid rise and fall of his chest quickened her pulse. He had a dangerous air about him, like he wanted to fuck her senseless. But instead of being frightened by it, it only turned her on even more.

"Take them off," he ordered again.

She shimmied them off in slow striptease, watching his reaction the entire time. His jaw tightened. His nostrils flared. His hands clenched into white-knuckled fists. But he stayed right where he was, his eyes never leaving her body.

He didn't touch her until she bent over to unzip her boots. "Did I say take them off?"

Oh, God, she could've come right there. He was turning into a better dom than she'd thought he'd be. "You want me to leave them on?"

"Yes." The one word came out as a strangled plea, and his body drew even tighter. Another thirty seconds passed with him doing nothing more than stare at her. At last, he unbuttoned his jeans and nodded toward her bed. "Lay down on the edge."

She did as she was told without breaking eye contact, her knees bent at the edge of the mattress. As his jeans came off, she propped herself up on her elbows to get a better view. A long, thick bulge strained against his boxer briefs, and she unconsciously licked her lips. She couldn't wait to have him inside her.

He crawled over her, his underwear still on, and captured her mouth in a kiss that revealed the complex emotions brewing between them. Desire was first and foremost, raging and yet controlled. But as the kiss deepened, she discovered subtle hints of both fear and trust. She wound her arms around his neck and slowed things down until the fear vanished.

He lifted his head, his hands and knees still braced around her, and looked down at her in awe. One hand leisurely traced the valley of her breasts and the flat plane of her stomach. "You are so beautiful."

A warm glow spread over her, driving away any traces of her self-conscious insecurities.

The hand trailed back up to her breasts, then up her neck to her cheek. "Show me what you like."

The warm glow from before flared into the heat of embarrassment. It was one thing to surrender to his orders. It was another thing to call the shots on the seduction. She withdrew her arms and turned away.

"Touch yourself, Becca. Show me where you want my hands, my mouth. Teach me how you like to be touched."

Each request became firmer, more demanding, until he hit upon her craving to submit. It would've been simple to tell him to just put on a condom and fuck her, but there was something in his eyes that told her he wanted more than that. He wanted to learn the intricacies of what she yearned for. He wanted her to draw the boundaries of her comfort zone. But most important, he wanted to make her come.

With some hesitation, she brushed her fingers over one taut nipple. "I like to be touched here."

"Show me."

She tried to squirm away, but his knees locked around her hips in a vise. There was no escaping his demand. She drew tiny circles around the peak, gathering her courage until she grasped it between her fingers and twisted. Her sex clenched, and she drew in a sharp breath from the sting.

"So you like it rough, too?" Without waiting for her answer, he repeated the same motions with her other breast, first with his fingers and then with his mouth.

Sweat beaded along her hairline as each nip grew harder. It was like he was testing her to see how far she was willing to go. The ache in her lower pelvis began to throb, and her body strained against the tight confines of his. When she reached the point where her nipples burned, she cried out, "No more."

He placed a single kiss between her breasts before lifting his head again. "Where else?"

He wanted more? Wasn't this foreplay enough? And yet she found herself dragging her fingers lower to the place between her thighs. As she dipped her finger between the folds, she turned away again.

"Look at me as you touch yourself."

The order was as rough as a drill sergeant's, and her body jerked to attention. She met his gaze again and started to withdraw her hand.

"No, don't stop." Ethan guided her hand back. "Make yourself come."

Her cheeks burned, and she reached for excuses. Anything but that. "It's kind of hard to do that with your knees holding my thighs together."

"Easily remedied." He shifted his weight and wedged his knees between her lower thighs, spreading them apart. "Now do it."

Despite his insistence that she look at him, she couldn't overcome the uncomfortable sensation that paralyzed her. This was taking intimacy to a whole new level. She closed her eyes and found her clit with her fingers. The gentlest touch sent shivers through her body. She rubbed it slowly, working up her courage to let go of all restraint in front of him.

"That's it, Bec. Show me."

His words soothed her anxieties, and she pressed harder until her hips started to tighten.

"Beautiful," he whispered.

Another set of fingers joined hers. Ethan delved into the further recess of her sex with one finger, then two, finding her G-spot with ease. He matched the tempo of his strokes with hers, each one bringing her closer and closer to release.

But just as she stood on the brink of coming, another wave of embarrassment washed over her and held her back. She withdrew her hand.

"No, don't stop."

"I can't," she admitted in a quiet voice of defeat.

"Then let me finish." He pressed his thumb against her clit, as rough and demanding as the kiss that claimed her lips. His fingers pumped harder, deeper, until she finally shattered against him.

She'd barely come back down to earth in time to hear him ask, "Where are the condoms?"

"Nightstand."

He reached over and grabbed one, kicking his underwear off and nearly knocking over the nightstand with his impatience. The rip of the foil packet broke the silence, and he rolled it on over his thick cock. Without waiting for permission or even asking if he should continue, he plunged into her.

But by now, he probably knew she came harder when he called the shots.

Her body trembled from the size of him and the intensity of him stretching her inner walls. He wasted no time building on the lingering aftershocks of her last orgasm. His hips pumped to the same rhythm as his fingers had earlier, but his cock went deeper, stimulating all her sensitive areas.

Her hips rose off the mattress to meet each of his thrusts, the tension coiling tight and tighter inside her. She wrapped her legs around his waist, wanting more, eager to have him fill her completely. Her impending release ambushed her, and she bit her bottom lip to keep from coming.

"No, Bec, don't hold back." His thrusts quickened, and each word came out as a single breath. "Do you have any idea how fucking gorgeous you are when you come? Now come."

Her body rebelled against her and responded to his command. The intensity of the orgasm slammed into her with enough force to make her grit her teeth together. She tightened her hold on him with her arms and legs, so scared that if she let go, she'd drown. Wave after wave of pleasure pulsated through her, pulling her so deep into a dream world of bliss that she didn't even notice that he'd reached his climax until he cried out her name and collapsed on top of her.

Her heart hammered in her chest as she held him through the residual effects. The salty taste of sweat lingered on her lips with each kiss she placed on his damp forehead. Her arms and legs turned as limp as rubber bands from exhaustion, and when Ethan finally lifted his head, she let them fall to the side.

He gave her a crooked grin. "That was…"

"Yeah," she finished for him. Right now, her brain couldn't even come up with the right words to describe sex with him. Mind-blowing, awesome, incredible—they all fell short.

He gave her one more tender kiss before rising from the bed and disappearing into the bathroom. The door closed behind him, and a chill bathed her bare skin.

Now came the awkwardness of the aftermath. It would be one thing if this was a cut-and-dry hookup or sex with someone she was in a long-term relationship with, but Ethan fell squarely into that gray area.

And the worst part was, she didn't want this to be a one-night deal. Sex had only complicated the feelings she was developing for him, and if he didn't feel the same….

She removed her boots and drew the covers up to her shoulders before rolling over to her side, her back to the bathroom door. It would save her the humiliation of reading too much into this if all he wanted was a quick fuck.

A band of light appeared on the wall in front of her, widening until a shadow filled its center. Then it vanished, plunging the room back into darkness. She held her breath, waiting to see if he would just grab his things and leave.

Instead, the mattress shifted under his weight, and his hard body curled around hers. "Do you mind if I stay a bit longer?" he asked.

She shook her head and smiled. "No."

"Good, because I don't want to leave just yet." He draped his arm around her waist and pulled her closer to him.

Chapter Nine

Ethan awoke to the scent of Becca's perfume on the pillows and the sensation of a warm, soft body lying next to him. A faint light filtered in from behind her curtains, announcing the morning's arrival. He rubbed the sleep from his eyes to make sure this wasn't a dream. When the image of Becca lying next to him didn't disappear, his lips curled into a grin.

I could get used to this.

Her breathing was slow and calm, so different from the shaking gasps she'd drawn when he ordered her to touch herself. He still felt a little bad about pushing her like he did, but it was the only thing he could think of to overcome his anxiety about making love to a woman sober. He didn't want to ruin this chance by coming too soon or doing something she didn't like. But in the process, he discovered another side to her. The more he told her what to do, the more aroused she'd become, even if it meant pushing her comfort levels.

Definitely something to keep in mind for next time.

He caught himself as soon as the thought materialized. Next time? Jesus, he'd only slept with her once, and he was already planning the next time. But he couldn't deny the worsening hard-on he was getting from picturing what he'd do to her.

I've got to get out of here before I wake her up demanding seconds.

He slipped out of bed with the stealth of a ninja, a skill learned from one too many one-night stands, and found his clothes. But by the time he'd pulled his jeans on, he was second-guessing his decision to sneak out. She deserved better than that, especially after he'd asked her if he could stay.

He paused and ran his fingers over his head. He'd never asked to stay the night with anyone before, and yet, with her, he wanted to. *Shit, I'm in over my head.*

Coffee. I need coffee.

He didn't bother putting his shirt on as he went to the kitchen. The apartment was still messy from the party, but an air of still silence hung over it in the early morning hours. After searching the cabinets, he found what he needed to start a pot of coffee, and leaned on the counter while it brewed.

So, how do I handle this?

He liked her. A lot, actually. Enough to even consider staying in town long enough to see where their relationship went. She was pretty, smart, adventurous, sexy…

The throbbing returned to his groin, and he groaned. There was no way he'd be able to get through another one of those NA meetings without remembering how it felt to be buried inside her. It wasn't something he'd considered when he'd kissed her or accepted her invitation to take things to her bedroom. And he needed to go to those meetings, if only to stay accountable and not relapse.

As his stomach tied itself up in knots, he waited for the familiar craving to hit.

But this time, it wasn't as intense as before. Instead of being a herculean task, it was something a mere mortal like him could handle.

He drew in a deep breath and exhaled, the craving passing as he remembered the hurdles he'd overcome last night. Becca had helped him in his moment of weakness. She'd helped him find the music again. And she'd given him the first night of peaceful sleep in over a month. She'd been far more instrumental in his recovery than anything else, and the last thing he wanted to do was mess up things with her.

I'll just gauge her reaction when she wakes up and go from there.

"God, I could use some coffee now," a sleepy female voice said from the living room.

Ethan spun around just as Ari came into the kitchen. They both froze and stared at each other. Her eyes widened, her voice full of shock. "I know you."

He backed away. "Yeah, I'm Becca's friend."

"No, I know you." She pointed to the tattoo of the tiger curling down his right arm. "I'd recognize that tattoo anywhere."

Sweat prickled the back of his neck. He could've sworn he'd never met Becca's roommate until last night, but who knows how many stupid things he'd done when he was high?

"You're Ethan Kelly of Ravinia's Rejects."

Becca had warned him that Ari was a huge fan, but that

didn't give justice to the awe-like reverence that lit up her face as she continued to point to him. He half expected some pre-pubescent squealing to follow, but she managed to stand quietly where she was with her mouth still forming a perfect circle of surprise.

"Um, yeah." He dropped his forehead to his shoulder to wipe the perspiration from it. So far, his first encounter with a fan since going into hiding was off to a fucking fantastic start.

She dropped her arm and came closer. "I'm a huge fan."

"So Becca told me."

"She is, too. We both are."

He spied his jacket and helmet by the door and started calculating the best escape route. "Oh, really?"

Ari nodded, her eyes still star-struck. "I know all the words to all your songs."

"Funny, so do I."

She blinked several times, and the spell ended. "Oh my God, what am I thinking? I need to get my phone to take a picture with you."

Shit! The last thing he wanted was her selfie with him plastered all over social media. It would blow his cover.

She ran back to her room, and he made a break for the door. He didn't care that he was half dressed as he pressed the down button for the elevator half a dozen times. He needed to get away from her camera lens as quickly as possible.

The elevator dinged, and he ducked inside. Just as the doors were closing, Ari appeared in the hallway and turned in his direction.

A Seductive Melody

The elevator started its descent, and he banged his forehead against the wall in frustration. Not the way he wanted the morning to end, but there was no way around it. The familiar craving simmered in his veins and tempted him to dive back into the abyss. He curled his hands into fists and waited for it to pass before pulling his jacket on. He slipped out of the building without any difficulty. His motorcycle was parked where he'd left it down the street, and he sped off for his loft.

He was pulling his bike into the freight elevator when his phone buzzed. He pulled it out, thinking maybe it was Becca calling to ask where he was, but instead, Adam's number flashed on the screen. Disappointment flowed out with a sigh, and he clicked the answer button. "Hey, Adam."

"Don't 'hey' me. You've had us all worried sick."

"Oh, really?" he asked while unlocking the door of his apartment. His eldest brother sounded way too much like their dad when he was pissed off. "And why is that?"

"Because it's the first time you've bothered to answer any of our calls in the last twenty-four hours."

Ethan pulled his phone back and checked the call log. Sure enough, there were at least twenty missed calls from his family since yesterday. "Sorry, I had my phone on silent."

"You need to come up with a better excuse than that. I was about to fly out there to make sure you were still alive."

"I'm not Ty," he replied, his voice tight with irritation. "I'm staying clean, so you don't have to worry about that."

"Then why the hell weren't you answering your

phone?"

"I already told you why." He parked his bike along the wall by the door and hung his helmet on the hook above it.

"Why did you have your phone on silent?"

"Why do you and Mom feel the need to check in on me every few hours? I'm not helpless, you know."

The anger melted from Adam's voice, leaving genuine concern in its wake. "It's just because we're worried about you."

"Well, stop worrying so much, okay? I have a great support system here, and she's wonderful. She's kind, thoughtful, smart, and has enough nerve to smack me upside the head when I'm being an idiot. She's already helped me work through so much on the road to staying clean, so you can stop treating me like a child."

Silence hung in the air for a moment, and Ethan's stomach sank. When Adam was quiet like that, it meant he was dissecting something that was said.

"So, tell me more about this support system of yours."

He could just imagine his brother's response if he told him who Becca was. She still didn't have the most stellar reputation, even though she'd retired from her party girl ways years ago. She'd tried to protect his privacy, and now it was his chance to return the favor. "That's none of your fucking business."

"There's a nine a.m. flight to LaGuardia I can still make," Adam warned.

"Just cut me some slack. I'm not a kid anymore."

"No, but you are in a tough place right now."

"News flash, Adam—Hell's Kitchen has gone under

some serious gentrification, so it's not the shithole it used to be. You saw how much my loft cost."

"That's not what I meant, and you know it."

Ethan plopped down on the sofa and massaged his temple. Adam and his mom had no doubt researched narcotic recovery and probably already knew about the one-month speed bump. "Yes, I'm at the one-month mark, and yes, it's been tough, but if I need any help, I can call on Becca."

"So her name's Becca, huh?"

Damn it! Adam had somehow managed to weasel her name from him. "Yeah."

"And she lives in the city?"

"No, she lives in fuckin' New Jersey."

Instead of shutting his brother up, the comment only made Adam laugh. "Ah, the sarcasm's back in full force. Always a good sign."

"See? I'm fine. So lay off with the bedtime checks, okay?"

"Fine, and I'll tell Mom to back off, too, but don't be surprised if she calls wanting to know more about Becca."

A lump the size of the Wall Street bull formed in his throat. "Why?"

"Because it's the first time you've mentioned a woman who wasn't some chick you banged while you were on tour."

No, but there was last night...

"And from the sound of things," Adam continued, "you think very highly of her."

"Yeah, I like her. She's cool, but there's no need for Mom to start planning another wedding. In fact, it might be nice if you didn't mention Becca to her."

"Don't want to get her hopes up?"

"Yeah, something like that."

But the more he thought about it, the more he liked the idea of being linked with Becca, of spending more time with her outside the NA arena, of being called her boyfriend instead of just her friend. He just had to figure out the best way to handle the transition to that point.

"I won't mention it to Mom if you tell me where you were last night."

Damn it, his brother never gave up. But that didn't mean he'd have to tell him everything. "I was celebrating Rosh Hashanah."

"Rosh Hash—what the fuck?"

"*Shanah Tovah*, Adam." He hung up and made sure his phone was still on silent before slipping it back into his pocket.

***

"Becca, you have some serious explaining to do!"

Becca shot up in bed at the sound of her roommate's irate screech. The first thing she noticed was that she was still naked from last night. The second thing was the still-warm impression next to her from another person. The pleasant ache between her legs reminded her of the previous night's encounter.

Holy shit! I slept with Ethan Kelly.

Then another more worrisome thought followed. *Where is he?*

Becca yanked the sheets up over her chest as Ari burst into her bedroom. "Haven't you heard of knocking?"

Ari stood at the foot of her bed, arms crossed and

cheeks florid. "Oh my God. You fucked him?"

"No, I just suddenly decided to sleep naked next to a sexy man, but managed to keep my hands off of him."

"Damn it, Becca! You know how long I've had a crush on Ethan Kelly."

Becca rested her forehead in her hand. So the cat was out of the bag. "Funny. You seemed rather pissed off that he was even here last night."

"That was before I realized who he was."

"Um, sorry?"

"Don't bother lying to me." Ari plopped down on the edge of the bed, her arms still crossed. "Did you know?"

"Of course I knew, but he wanted to fly under the radar, and I respect that."

"But I'm your best friend. You could've at least told me."

Becca checked the clock. 7:14 a.m. Way too early to be having this conversation on her day off. "Speaking of Ethan, where is he?"

The redness in Ari's cheeks spread to her ears and neck, and her ramrod straight posture wilted. She turned away, twirling a strand of blond hair around her finger. "Well, um, I think I scared him away."

Becca jumped to her knees, still clutching the sheet to her chest and ignoring the blast of cool air that bathed her bare ass. "What happened?"

Ari gave her a nervous laugh and moved on to a new segment of her hair to twirl. "Well, I smelled the coffee he was making, found him in the kitchen with his shirt off—by the way, he's way hotter in person than in any of his photos. No wonder why you wanted to keep him all to yourself."

"Out with it, Ari."

She released her hair and threw her hands down in her lap with an exasperated sigh. "I guess I went a little crazy fan-girl on him."

"And then?"

"He freaked out and bolted."

"Damn it, Ari! I expected better from you, what with Gabe being a movie star and all."

"I'm sorry, but he was there—in our kitchen—half naked. I just, you know, lost it."

Becca wrapped the sheet around her and climbed out of bed, searching for her phone in the mess of clothes on the floor. Once she found it, she dialed his number and counted the rings before it went to voice mail.

Shit!

She hung up without leaving a message and sank back down on her bed. She'd try again later, and if she couldn't reach him by phone, she hoped she could catch him at the next NA meeting and apologize for her roommate's behavior.

Ari sat next to her, her head still bowed. "Sorry, Becca. I didn't mean to scare him off."

"It's fine. I'm sure I'll get hold of him and explain everything."

Ari nodded, then asked, "So, how was it?"

Now it was Becca's turn to blush. "Wow."

"Wow?"

"Yes, definitely wow."

Chapter Ten

"Rebecca, may I please have a word with you?"

A dozen pairs of eyes zeroed in on her after Elaine made her request at the end of the weekly staff meeting, all of them wondering why the lowly assistant had been singled out by the editor-in-chief.

Becca wiped her palms on her skirt and nodded. "Sure, Elaine."

"In my office." She beckoned her to follow her down the hall to the corner office with breathtaking views of Midtown. "Close the door behind you."

Becca did as she was told and waited for Elaine to sit down behind her desk before taking a seat across from her. Her mouth was so dry, she doubted she'd be able to respond to anything her boss said, and she wished she'd brought the bottle of water from her cubicle with her to the meeting.

"You're been here since January, correct?"

"Yes."

Elaine put on a pair of designer reading glasses and skimmed over some of the papers on her desk while she spoke. "And while I appreciate you speaking up in our meetings with suggestions for articles, I don't think you've firmly grasped who *Moderne*'s audience is. Our reader is a young, modern female who wants to stay on top of all the trends, be it fashion, beauty, or men. She is not interested in the need to educate schoolgirls in third world countries."

Oh great, I'm about to get fired.

Becca curled her fingers into the nubby knitted fabric of her skirt. "Yes, Elaine."

The editor set down her papers and removed her glasses to pinch the bridge of her nose. "I know you would like to write more serious articles, but that's not what we do here. I'm far more interested in what you can give me through your social connections."

Becca's spine stiffened, and her fear morphed into a mixture of outrage and confusion. She struggled to keep her voice calm as she asked, "My connections?"

"Yes, you're Becca Shore, party girl extraordinaire and heiress to a fortune," Elaine explained with a flourish. "You know people my readers are eager to learn about. You can provide *Moderne* with the juicy celebrity gossip that will make issues fly off the newsstand. Why do you think I agreed to take you on?"

A bitter taste filled her mouth, but she kept it closed.

Elaine leaned forward, arms on her desk. "Surely, you must know something we can use."

How about the fact I screwed Ethan Kelly last week? I bet your readers would love to find out what he's like in the bedroom.

But she wasn't the fuck-and-tell type. Not to mention, she was too busy trying to convince him to trust her. He hadn't made any effort to contact her since he ran out of her apartment Friday morning.

She kept her face blank and shook her head. "Not at the moment."

Elaine's face hardened, and she sat back in her chair. "Well, then consider that your assignment, Rebecca. We're getting into the holiday season, and I expect with your family's connections, you'll have your pick of parties to attend. If someone important so much as sneezes, I want to hear about it."

So, I'm being regulated to being a celebrity spy.

She squeezed her hands into fists to keep from telling Elaine no. As crappy as this job was, it was a job that paid her modest bills, and the last thing she needed was to get canned. If she had no income, she'd be forced to crawl back to her father and concede to his demands. "I'll see what I can do."

"Excellent. I look forward to seeing your reports." Elaine turned her attention to her computer and dismissed Becca with a wave of her hand.

Becca retreated to her cubicle, unable to ease the sick feeling in her stomach. The only reason she'd gotten this job was because of who she used to be, and now she was in danger of losing it. Her dream of becoming a respected journalist seemed further away than ever.

She pulled out her phone and dialed Ari's number. "Can you get away for lunch? I really need someone to talk to."

"Sure. Want to meet at Le Cirque? I know the maître d', and he can squeeze us in."

Becca winced at the thought of the pricy check that would entail, but brushed it off with the excuse that she needed the splurge. "Sure. Meet you there at noon?"

"I'm in a meeting until twelve-thirty, so make it one. See you then."

***

Later, lunch still sat like a lead brick in the pit of Becca's stomach as she left work. She'd spent two hours brainstorming with Ari about how she could save her job without becoming a social pariah, and nothing seemed feasible.

Of course, it didn't help that Ari kept bringing up her relationship with Ethan. It was only when Becca threatened to publish photos of Gabe in braces and headgear that Ari backed off. Some things didn't need to be made public, and Ethan Kelly was one of them.

She hurried down the street to the nearest subway station. The train was waiting at the track when she reached the stairs leading to the platform. She ran down to catch it, only to feel something crack under her feet. Her ankle rolled, and she stumbled down the last few steps, praying she didn't make a face plant on the concrete. By the time she caught her balance, the doors had closed.

She glanced down at the broken heel of her shoe and cursed. If they'd been real Jimmy Choos instead of knockoffs, she would've made the train. Now she was left with a ruined pair of shoes and would be late for her NA meeting.

She hobbled over to the nearest bench and fished through her bag for the tiny tube of super-glue she kept there for emergencies. There was a time in her life when she would've tossed the shoes in the garbage and bought a new pair, but the cost of lunch had set her back far enough on her finances that new shoes were out of the question. For now, she had to patch the heel back on and pray it would last until she got home and could apply some stronger glue.

Her ankle was starting to swell by the time she snuck into the meeting. She didn't even bother looking for Ethan and opted for the closest open chair. Instead of listening to the other members, her mind whirled around her own predicament. She could either become a rat or end up at the mercy of her father again. Just the idea of living under his constant scrutiny was enough to revive the familiar craving.

When she was high, she didn't care what he thought about her. His criticism rolled off like splashes on her favorite Burberry rain boots. But if she went back to him, she'd have to admit she was wrong about the choices she'd made, and he'd be completely insufferable.

It's better to be poor and hungry than be tempted to get high again.

It was a revelation she'd come to two years ago, and it gave her the strength to quiet the craving. If she lost her job at *Moderne*, she could find something else to do. Bartend. Wait tables. Maybe even see if she could get on at the public relations firm where Ari worked. Besides, if she were broke, she'd think more than twice about dropping twenty dollars every time she wanted to get high.

The meeting drew to a close, and she met Ethan's gaze across the room. Her breath caught from the intensity of his stare, and she squirmed in her seat from the memories of him ordering her to touch herself. Part of her wanted to flee before he caught her just to avoid the awkward "So, about the other night" conversation, but the predatory heat in his gray eyes almost forbade her to leave without speaking to him first.

And he knew what a sucker she was when he ordered her to do something.

She stayed in her seat and waited for him while the others wandered out of the basement.

He wove this way through the crowd until he stood in front of her, his hands buried in his pockets. Even dressed in a faded T-shirt and worn jeans, he was sexy. "Hi."

"Hi," she repeated, not coming up with anything better to say.

He rocked back and forth on his feet before sitting in the chair next to her. "Becca, I…." His voice trailed off, and he looked away.

Her throat tightened. This was where he was going to give her the "Thanks for the other night, but I think we should just be friends" spiel. And she deserved it. After all, she'd been the one to invite him back to her bed when he was still in a precarious position of his recovery.

He rubbed the back of his neck and turned back to her. "Can we go to the café and talk?"

"Sure," she said with an extra dose of false cheer in her voice.

When she stood, though, the throbbing in her ankle roared to life and sent a jolt of pain up her leg. She gasped and lurched forward.

Ethan caught her, his brows drawing together in worry. "What's wrong?"

"These stupid shoes." She sat back down and took off the offending shoe. The strong glue had failed, and now the heel dangled by a thin strip of fake leather. "I twisted my ankle on the way over here."

"Let me take a look." He knelt in front of her to examine her ankle. "You know, this is the second time I've seen you stumble in those heels. You should think about sturdier footwear."

"And risk not being fashionable? Never!"

His warm hands caressed her calf and slid down to the swollen joint. The sensation awakened her desire and brought back memories of his hands on other parts of her body. And despite the fact that his inspection of her ankle was far from sexual, she grew more and more turned on with every gentle squeeze.

"It doesn't look broken," he said and looked back at her. He paused, and as though he read her desire, his mouth curled up in a sexy grin that made her slick with anticipation. "Maybe we should just go back to your place?"

"Are you ready to handle Ari?"

"Good point." He rose and scooped her up in his arms. "My place it is."

Her tongue tripped over itself in embarrassment. "You don't need to carry me."

"And you don't need to be walking on that ankle." He climbed up the stairs with the same brisk pace as he did with empty arms. "Besides, it'll give me a chance to play knight in shining armor."

"I'm not a damsel in distress."

"No, but I definitely don't mind." He carried her to his motorcycle. "Do you think you'll be able to ride?"

"I should."

"Then strap on your helmet." He handed it to her and put on his own.

She'd been so flustered from his chivalry that she'd forgotten he wanted to go back to his place until he headed west toward Hell's Kitchen. Warning bells sounded in the back of her mind. If she went back to his place, she risked getting naked with him again. But she rationalized that she could exercise some self-control around Ethan Kelly, and knowing where he lived would be important in case she needed to check in on him.

He pulled up to a renovated warehouse and turned off the engine. "Stay on," he ordered as he pushed her and the bike inside and onto the freight elevator.

"Don't trust your neighbors?" she teased.

"Not with this." The elevator opened at the top floor and he paused to unlock the single door in front of them. "Sorry about the mess."

Scattered papers covered the furniture and tables, and a collection of empty soda cans gathered on the kitchen counter. But as he carried her across the room, she discovered the papers were sheet music, and each one had notes drawn on the scales.

The loft had the industrial vibe so popular with converted warehouses. Exposed brick lined the walls, and large windows offered her a glimpse of the city lights shimmering off the Hudson River. The kitchen was a sleek combination of black lacquer and stainless steel, and a black metal staircase led to the open bedroom above.

He cleared a space on his sofa and set her down there before gathering the sheet music into neat piles. "I've been, um, kind of on a binge lately."

"What kind of binge?" Her heart pounded, and she checked for track marks along the tattooed vein on his left arm.

He held up his hands and shook his head. "No, no, no—not that kind of a binge." He gathered a few more stacks of music sheets and placed them on the grand piano in the middle of the room. "A music binge. Ever since I left your place, I've had one song after another pop into my mind, and I was trying to write them all down before I lost them."

"So that's what you were doing all weekend? Composing new material?"

"Um, yeah." He rubbed the back of his neck again and focused on her ankle. "Let me get you some ice."

He disappeared into the kitchen area of the loft and filled a plastic bag full of crushed ice from the dispenser in his refrigerator door. Then he wrapped it in a dish towel and gently placed it on her ankle. "Too cold?"

"No, it's fine." She shifted back on the sofa to make room for him to sit down. "Tell me about these new songs."

"It's been crazy, Bec. It was like—*bam!*—a floodgate opening up. I think I've written enough new material to record a whole album. I've hardly slept all weekend, and tonight was the first time I've stepped out of my apartment since I came home Friday morning."

Hmm...I wonder what Elaine would say if I told her Ethan Kelly was moving on without the rest of Ravinia's Rejects.

He flashed her a sheepish grin. "I suppose I ought to apologize for not calling you back, but I...."

So that's why he didn't call. "It's fine."

"No, it's not." He got up and paced in front of her, his hands jammed into his pockets again. "I should've called." He paused and added, "I wanted to call."

"Don't worry, Ethan. I understand. After weeks of writer's block, I know you didn't want to disrupt the flow."

"Yeah, but I didn't want to hurt you, either." He sat back down on the sofa and took her hand in his. "What I mean to say is, I really enjoyed the other night, and I'm hoping I didn't fuck things up by leaving like I did or not calling."

"I can understand why you left. Ari can be a little…intense."

"I was terrified she'd post a photo of me on Facebook or something like that. You of all people know how hard it is to hide once the paparazzi finds out where you are."

She nodded. Those days seemed like a distant memory, but she remembered what it was like to walk out of the gym to the flash of cameras trying to capture her at her most sweaty. "So what are you saying, Ethan?"

"This." He leaned forward and kissed her until she forgot about everything but the pressure of his lips against hers. He moved slowly, seeking her permission to continue, and when she granted it, he swept in and deepened the kiss. His arms wrapped around her, and the passion of his embrace aroused her hunger more than a four-course meal at a five-star restaurant.

She kissed him back, her hands reaching for him, exploring everything she could about him. The taste of his tongue as it entwined with hers. The subtle cedar in his cologne mixing with the scent of fabric softener on his shirt. The carved ripples of his abs and biceps. Before she could stop herself, she was falling back on the sofa and pulling him with her.

Thankfully, he was thinking clearly enough to pull back before they both got naked. He leaned over her, his arms like iron bars on either side of her chest, and struggled to catch his breath. "Becca, I want you so badly."

"Then what's the holdup?" She reached to pull him back to down into another kiss, but he shook her off.

"No, I mean, I want more than just sex. I like you. You get me."

"So what are you suggesting?"

"You know—the normal dating stuff. Dinner." He placed a simple peck on the corner of her mouth. "A movie." Another one on the tip of her nose. "Then maybe dessert."

He gazed down at her, the hunger in his eyes matched only by the tense, yet hopeful smile.

For a supposedly jaded rocker, his request was refreshingly innocent and sincere. She licked her lips and wrapped her arms around his neck. "You know how much I like dessert."

"Damn, Bec, when you say it that way…." This time, he didn't shake her off when she pulled him back into another kiss. Without breaking contact with her mouth, he scooped her up in his arms again and carried her up the metal staircase to the bed.

He laid her down and grinned. "Speaking of dessert, ever since Thursday night, I've had a craving for honey." He leaned in closer and added in a low rumble, "But only if I get to lick it off of you."

Another shiver of delight coursed down her spine at the thought of his tongue exploring her body. "Do you happen to have any?

"I'll add it to my shopping list. Right now, you're sweet enough."

As they stripped off their clothes, she indulged in the fantasy of how easy it would be to fall in love with Ethan Kelly.

Chapter Eleven

The doorbell interrupted Becca while she was applying her final coat of mascara. She glanced down at the time on her phone.

Shit! He's early.

She made quick work of her lashes and applied a coat of sheer lip color before checking her reflection in the mirror. Not as perfect as she would've liked, but acceptable. The vintage knee-length, fifties-styled ice blue dress made her eyes pop, and the glittering beadwork added just the right sparkle for the occasion.

Ari was opening the front door when Becca exited her bedroom. Her roommate was dressed in a simple red sheath that clung to her petite curves and boasted a revealing slit from ankle to hip. Unlike her, Ari didn't "rent the runway" or explore secondhand stores for clothes. She owned the designer dress. "Hey, Ethan."

Becca released the pent-up breath. In the nearly two months she and Ethan had been dating, Ari had overcome her adolescent adoration and saw him simply as Becca's boyfriend, and Ethan was much more relaxed when he hung out at her apartment.

"Hey, Ari. You look nice."

He stepped into the apartment, and Becca's pulse quickened. He'd always been sexy with his rough around the edges, bad-boy air. But dressed in a tux, he'd become downright irresistible. The satin lapels matched his short, slicked-back black hair, and the lines accentuated his broad shoulders and lean waist.

I want to drag him back to the bedroom and muss him up right away.

He turned to her and froze, his mouth slightly ajar. "Wow, Bec. You look great."

Her cheeks grew warm, and she lowered her eyes with a shy smile. "You clean up pretty nicely yourself."

"Not all cleaned up." He lifted his trousers enough to show the polished metal-studded motorcycle boots. "I had to retain some bit of myself."

"You rebel." She slipped her arms through his. "So are you telling me that we're taking your bike to the Museum Gala?"

He laughed, never taking his eyes off of her. "No, I can spring for a taxi." Then he waved to Ari. "We'll see you there."

Ari waved and rushed back to her bathroom to finish getting ready. Her roommate didn't have a date for the event, and for a moment, Becca thought about inviting her to share a cab with them. That thought flew out of her mind, though, the second Ethan pulled her into his arms and kissed her.

"You look like a sexy snow queen."

"Are you suggesting I launch into that Idina Menzel song?"

A Seductive Melody

He pulled back, his face scrunched up in horror, and laughed again. "No, don't. Ty's sister and her little girl joined us on tour around the time the movie came out, and all I heard for days was that song."

The mirth faded, and his gaze grew distant, the same way it always did when he spoke of Ty. He rubbed his left forearm over the place where his best friend's name was tattooed, the way he always did when a craving hit him.

Becca cupped his cheek in one hand and placed a kiss on the other to pull him from his somber mood. "Let's go before they run out of virgin cocktails."

The American Museum of Natural History's annual gala was one of New York City's hottest social events, and she didn't want to miss a thing, especially since Elaine was still hounding her for more celebrity gossip. She managed to unearth a few gems during the New Yorker Festival and NYC Food and Wine Week last month, but this would be the first time she'd be surrounded by enough big names to land a good story.

Of course, the breakout story was escorting her to the event. Ethan's turnaround and comeback never ceased to amaze her. He'd written fourteen songs since Rosh Hashanah and was working with some set musicians to record them for a solo album. All this was being done in secret, but when the news would eventually get out, it would set the music world buzzing.

But no matter how many times she was tempted to be the one to write that story, she refused to betray his trust in her.

The taxi drove across Central Park and dropped them off at the Museum of Natural History. Growing up, she'd heard stories from her parents about the extravagant event that took place under the shadows of the blue whale and the T-rex, but this was her first time attending. And it was all due to Ethan. She'd mentioned wanting to go a few weeks ago when they were touring the exhibits, and he surprised her a few hours later with tickets.

Once inside the rotunda, they found their way to the bar. Ethan ordered her usual club soda with lime and got a Coke for himself. A scan of the room identified dozens of her parents' friends and the elite of New York society. Celebrities from stage and screen mingled among them, adding extra energy to the excitement in the room.

Becca made her way through the crowd, stopping to chat with people she knew. She introduced Ethan as her boyfriend, using his first name only. Every time she said it, though, a little rush of glee struck her. She still couldn't believe this charismatic, sexy man was dating her. He could've had his pick of any of the actresses or models in the room, but his fingers remained firmly entwined with hers, and his attention never wavered from her.

How did I get so lucky?

She was floating on cloud nine until she heard someone say her name and turned around.

***

Despite his aversion to crowds and large parties, Ethan was glad he'd gotten the tickets for the Gala. Becca lit up the room. It was more than the icicle blue dress that hugged her full breasts and accentuated her curvy hips. It was the way she worked the crowd—smiling, laughing, engaging with complete strangers and making them feel at ease. The Gala awakened the partying side of her that had been dormant for years, but her maturity tempered it with a sophistication he wished he could replicate.

Initially, he'd held her hand to soothe his anxiety about being recognized at such an important event. The craving to get high and forget about his jitters ambushed him several times during the first half hour, but each time, he looked inside himself and found a way to push it aside. As his nerves eased, he held on to her hand as a symbol of pride. He'd caught the admiring glances some of the other men had thrown her way as she weaved through the crowd, and a flame of jealousy roared to life within him. She was his girlfriend, and he wanted to make that very clear to anyone who met them.

All was going well until Becca turned around and came face to face with a tall, elegant older woman.

The color drained from Becca's face, and it was her turn to squeeze his fingers for support. "Claire."

His gut knotted with worry, but he resisted the urge to swoop in and rescue her, especially with so many people there to witness them making a scene.

Claire started to reach for her like she wanted to hug her, but then lowered her arms and drew back. "It's so wonderful running into you here, Becca," she said, her shaking words mirroring the nervous smile on her face. "And who's this?"

"My boyfriend, Ethan," she replied, just as she'd had all evening.

The tension between the two women smothered the joy from earlier. Claire kept looking as though she was waiting for Becca's permission to continue, but Becca looked like she was a breath away from bolting. She trembled beside him, her grip threatening to cut off the circulation in his hand.

The uneasy silence that stretched between them gave him a chance to study Claire closer. She was tall and lithe, the few lines around her eyes hinting at her age, but the glowing beauty of her skin made it difficult to guess. Her honey-colored hair cascaded over her shoulder in glossy waves, and her strapless evening gown created cleavage that most men probably wouldn't be able to turn away from. But there was something about her that seemed vaguely familiar.

"Is there any chance you've changed your mind about Thanksgiving?" Claire asked. "Jacob told me you had plans, but your father and I would love to have you at the table."

"Claire, you know I can't." Becca's attention shifted to someone behind Claire, and she stumbled back, her hand slipping from his. "Excuse me. I have to go to the ladies' room."

Claire's face tightened with anguish as Becca fled in the direction of the Asian Mammals Exhibit, but it wasn't until she spoke that Ethan believed it was genuine. "I'm terribly sorry you had to witness that. Even though she's as stubborn as her father, I still have hope they can make amends."

That one sentence made him realize there was a whole side to Becca he didn't know. They'd been together for almost two months, but during that time, she'd hardly ever mentioned her family. And now that he'd gained a hint as to why, he became determined to unravel the whole story.

"I'll see what I can do," he said to Claire a moment

before an older man with the same blue-green eyes as Becca came up and put his arm around her waist. Ethan nodded in acknowledgment to the man he assumed was Becca's father, and turned around to find his date.

The music signaling the Gala attendees to make their way downstairs to the dinner tables sounded, and Ethan found himself fighting against the tide of humanity heading in that direction. Once he broke free, he searched for the nearest ladies' room.

He found Becca leaning against the stone walls outside the restroom, her head tilted up toward the ceiling and her eyes closed. The calm, collected woman he'd always known seemed on the verge of having a panic attack. Her ragged breaths flowed in and out with enough force to shake her body. Her hands clenched and unclenched, and a sheen of perspiration covered her pale face.

He approached her with caution, afraid any sudden movement might send her over the edge. "Talk to me, Bec," he said when he got close enough to talk in a hushed voice.

Her eyes snapped open, wide with fear. "Ethan, I...." She exhaled with a sigh and closed them again. "I'm sorry you had to see that."

It wasn't the answer he was hoping for, but she seemed to pull herself together. Her breathing slowed, and some of the color returned to her cheeks.

He stood in front of her and leaned against the wall. "Funny. Claire said the same thing."

He waited for her to expound on the encounter, but all she did was crack open one wary eye.

"So, what's the story?" he asked, determined to get to

the bottom of the situation.

"Nothing."

"Bullshit, Becca. I watched you all night long, and something about that woman made you lose your cool."

"Just drop it, okay?"

"No, I'm not going to let up until you at least tell me who she is."

She let out another heavy sigh, this one full of exasperation, and opened both eyes. She continued to look up at the ceiling while her body squirmed and the toe of her shoe tapped against the floor. "Claire is my stepmother."

"What's your problem with her?"

"Nothing at all. I like her. She's the only mom I've ever known, and she's probably the kindest person you'll ever meet."

"Then why did you run away from her?"

The tapping of her toe quickened, and Becca bit her bottom lip. "It wasn't her I was running away from. It was my father."

A protective urge rose inside him so quickly, he forgot to breathe. His vision clouded with red vengeance. What had that asshole done to her to make her this terrified? "Why?"

She pushed off the wall, still avoiding his gaze. "Listen, Ethan, it's complicated, and I don't want to drag you into it."

"Too late." He corralled her back against the wall, his arms fencing her in. "I'm your boyfriend, remember? I'm already involved."

She finally looked at him, and the tension in her face

softened into affection. "I know, Ethan, but—"

"No buts." He tilted her chin up. "Now, what happened between you and your father?"

She chewed her bottom lip and tried to turn away, but every time she did, he guided her attention back to him. After a minute of trying to avoid his question, she said in a quiet voice, "I avoid my father because he's my trigger."

The air whooshed out of his lungs, and the angry rigidity in his arms slackened. "Are you planning on taking a hit?"

Her face drew up in disgust. "Absolutely not! I've been clean for too long to relapse just from something like this."

"Then tell me why he's your trigger."

She opened her mouth, everything in her body screaming in protest, but he stopped her by placing his index finger on her lips. "You helped me when I was in a bad place. Now it's my turn."

That brief glimpse of gratitude bloomed in her eyes, and he knew he'd done the right thing pressing the issue.

She took a deep breath, her toe still tapping its rapid beat, and then grew still as she exhaled. "My mother was a heroin addict, too. She overdosed when I was a baby, so I have no memory of her. But my father did. And it became apparent at a very early age that I was just like her."

Becca played with one of the tiny beads on her skirt as she continued. "My father thought that if he controlled everything, if he kept me on the straight and narrow, I wouldn't end up like my mother. What started out as a gesture of concern became smothering. If I walked in a minute past my ridiculously early curfew, I was punished.

If I made a B instead of an A, I never heard the end of it. If I had a hair out of place or gained a couple of pounds, I was lectured on how my appearance reflected negatively on the family. By the time I got to my teen years, I lived in constant fear of him finding some fault in me. And he always found something wrong.

"My relief came through a skiing accident. I broke my ankle and got Percocet for the first time. And oh my god, what an epiphany it was. When I was on the meds, I didn't care about anything. I could be in my father's company and not suffer the gut-wrenching panic that I'd do something wrong. It was the release I'd been searching for, and for once in my life, I felt peace."

Ethan's heart squeezed a little tighter as he listened, knowing all too well what she was talking about.

"I went through the first bottle, then the second, then the third. My ankle healed, but the craving never went away. I started raiding my parents' and grandparents' medicine cabinets for more. I faked a back injury. I found contacts at school who could supply me with more Percocet. But when the cost got too high, I was introduced to the cheaper fix from heroin."

She gave a rueful laugh. "I'd been using for well over a year before Claire noticed the track marks. Daddy had a shit fit when he found out and forced me into rehab, but we both know what happened next."

He recalled her story of how she almost died before going clean for good.

"The night I overdosed, I was at a charity event like this with my parents. My father criticized my dress for being too revealing, so I retreated to the bathroom and shot up so I could make it through the rest of the evening." She drew in another deep breath. "The rest is history."

Part of Ethan physically ached for her. He'd always wondered why someone as privileged as Becca would turn to drugs, but he'd just assumed it had been out of boredom or to fit in with her fellow partiers. "So that's why you avoid him?"

She nodded and stared at the toes of her now-still shoes. "I realized during my second stint in rehab that I'd be better off not dealing with the constant pressure he put on me, so I cut myself off from him. I have lunch with Claire once in a while, and I talk to my younger brother, Jacob, at least once a week, but I haven't spoken to my father in almost two years."

He couldn't imagine cutting himself off from his family. Yes, his old man had given him a hard time growing up, but he'd also encouraged Ethan's love of music and stood behind his decision to forgo college and hit the road with the band. And as much as his mother and brothers annoyed him with their constant need to check on him, he knew it was because they cared. He was thankful to have a large family that gave a damn about him.

Now he just had to help Becca realize her family did, too.

"So what's this about Thanksgiving?" he asked.

"Jacob called a couple of weeks ago and asked me to join the family at our cabin in the Catskills for Thanksgiving. I tried to tell him no, but he wouldn't back down until I at least said I'd think about it."

"Sounds like both he and Claire would like for you to be part of the family again."

"Yeah, but look what a mess I became when I saw my father across the room. Now imagine what would happen if I was sitting at the table with him for an hour or more."

He cradled her hand in his own and kissed her knuckles before pressing it against the spot in his chest where his heart beat. "I'll be there with you."

Her lips parted in surprise. "Really, you don't have to do that. My family is fucked up, and I'm sure you'd much rather spend Thanksgiving with yours."

"They'll understand." He closed the space between them until their foreheads touched. "Please, Bec, let me help you the way you helped me. I'm not suggesting you have dinner with your father every Friday night, but I think we can get through Thanksgiving dinner together."

Her eyes glistened with tears, but she managed to blink them back before they fell. She squeezed his hand in return. "Okay, then. Together."

"Good." He took a step back and looped her arm through his. "Why don't we tell Claire she'll need to set the table for two more guests?"

Becca shook her head and gave him the first smile he'd seen since she'd bumped into her stepmother. "Oh, no. Not tonight. I'll text her tomorrow. Right now, I just want to forget about my father and enjoy the rest of the evening with you."

"I can live with that." They went downstairs and joined Ari at a table, not bringing it up again for the rest of dinner.

Chapter Twelve

"I'm going to be sick."

"My driving isn't that horrible," Ethan teased as he drove the rented Mercedes G-class SUV along the snow-covered country road.

She only wished she could blame it on being in a car for the last two hours. The closer they got to her father's cabin, the tighter the knots in her stomach squeezed. In a couple of miles, she'd be ready to hurl.

As though he knew what she was worried about, he reached over and wrapped his hand around hers. "It'll be okay, Becca. We can get through this."

Not her. *We*. For some strange reason, he was in this for the long haul, and her heart did a little flop. Every other guy she'd dated had been so terrified of her father, they'd take off at the first sign of his presence. But Ethan had not only agreed to come to the Catskills for Thanksgiving dinner, but for the whole weekend. She just hoped that he wouldn't come to his senses halfway through and say, "Forget this."

"Let's find something to distract you," he suggested.

Yeah, something besides how good it would feel to shoot up and block out this whole weekend.

"Um, how did your last recording session go?"

"Really well." He grinned, his eyes never leaving the road. The snow fell heavier as the SUV wound up the mountainside.

"Care to expand on that?"

"I played with some new riffs, and it added a whole new level to the song."

They hit a patch of ice under the snow, and the rear end of the SUV fishtailed. Becca gripped the door handle and clamped her jaw shut, so scared that if she opened her mouth, she'd puke. When her pulse returned to normal, she asked, "How so?"

"It created more depth." He slowed the car down as the incline grew steeper. "It's strange doing this solo album. On one hand, I still miss collaborating with Ty and the other guys, but on the other hand, it's so freeing. I'm finally getting to make music I like, to record the songs that speak to me."

"Any chance I can hear a demo soon?"

He shook his head, just as he had every other time she'd asked. "Not until it's ready."

"And when will that be? When you launch it on iTunes?"

He laughed. "No, Bec, I'll let you hear it before then. I'm just still trying to sound it out, if you know what I mean. Sort of like how you don't let your editor see your rough notes for a story. You wait until you think it's polished before turning it in. I feel the same way about my music."

The GPS dinged, and he slowed down to a crawl. "Is

this where I turn?"

She nodded, the queasiness reviving tenfold.

The car passed the metal gates that marked the beginning of her family's property and inched up the narrow lane through firs that bowed down under the weight of the snow. She'd almost talked Ethan out of going this morning when the weather report called for a winter storm in the Catskills, but he'd shrugged it off by telling her he grew up in Chicago and could handle the snow. The trees cleared to reveal the sprawling Arts and Crafts style home surrounded by three smaller bungalows.

Ethan let out a low whistle. "I thought you said it was a cabin. Unless, of course, you were referring to one of those smaller ones there."

She gave him a playful shove and found herself chuckling. "You should see the beach house in the Hamptons."

"I have no room to talk. You should see my family's 'cabin' on Geneva Lake. It had to accommodate all nine of us growing up."

"This was actually one of my great-grandfather's first hotels. When the area fell out of fashion in the seventies, we turned it into a vacation home."

Ethan parked the SUV behind the other cars and turned to her. "Ready?"

"No," she whimpered. She doubted she'd ever be ready to deal with her father.

"Come on, Bec, you're strong enough to get through this. I'll be on my best behavior and charm the socks off them."

She wished she could agree with him. She wasn't sure

which one of them her father would attack first. At least Ethan had toned the rocker look down for the weekend. The cream-colored fisherman's sweater he wore looked like something from an L.L. Bean catalog—perfect for a rustic weekend in the mountains. It covered his tattoos, and even though he hadn't shaved this morning, his stubble appeared neatly groomed.

But he wore his favorite boots, much to her delight. She was grateful he was willing to fit in with her preppy family, but still retain part of himself.

She gathered her courage along with her weekend bag and nodded. "Let's go."

The warm scents of roasted turkey and maple-glazed sweet potatoes greeted her when she opened the front door. She breathed it in and focused on how tasty the meal would be instead of how torturous. "Hello?"

Mrs. Cordero, her parents' housekeeper, appeared in the foyer with outstretched arms. "Rebecca, you made it." She pulled her into a vicious hug that expelled the air from her lungs. "How are you, *mai*?"

Becca unraveled her scarf while she caught her breath. "Good, and you?"

"I can't complain." She took Becca's coat and turned to Ethan. "And who is this? *¡Estás bueno!*"

Ethan grinned at the middle-aged Puerto Rican woman batting her eyelashes at him and flirted right back. "You first, *bonita*."

Mrs. Cordero's plump cheeks reddened. She pulled Becca aside and whispered, "I like him already. You should keep him."

Becca chuckled. "I think I might."

A Seductive Melody

It was becoming easier and easier to fall in love with Ethan Kelly. She couldn't help but grin like a goofy, lovestruck teenager whenever she thought of him. He could be moody and reserved at times, but he was always there when she needed him. Thoughtful and intelligent, he knew how to soothe her soul when it was troubled and how to make her body writhe with pleasure. But most important, he made her feel like the most beautiful woman in the world whenever he looked at her.

"Ethan, this is Mrs. Cordero. She's been with my family as long as I can remember. *Mami*, this is my boyfriend, Ethan."

His chest puffed up when she introduced him. "A pleasure to meet you, Mrs. Cordero."

"Oh, yes, I like him." She giggled behind her hand before waving for them to follow her. "You're just in time for dinner."

Mrs. Cordero ran the vacation home the same way she did her parents' home in Manhattan—with well-ordered discipline tempered by her jovial mood. It was no surprise at all to find her orchestrating the holiday dinner down to the precise second Becca's father requested. When they arrived in the oversized dining room, two maids were already placing the appetizers in front of the guests. She left Becca and Ethan to give the maids a few more orders in Spanish before chasing them back into the kitchen ahead of her.

The warm, affectionate welcome of the housekeeper contrasted sharply with the cool, dissecting one she received from her family. Her father sat at the head of the table, his hard blue-green gaze picking her apart before shifting to Ethan. The rest of the family—aunts, uncles, cousins—sat quietly in the seats as though they were waiting for permission to eat.

Claire stood from her place on the opposite end of the table and gave Becca a slight hug. "Becca, I'm so glad you and your boyfriend made it. We were getting worried."

"Yes, you're three minutes late, Rebecca," her father said in a steely voice. "You and your guest are holding up dinner."

Two faults already, and I haven't even sat down. She forced a genteel smile on her face and followed Claire to the two empty seats at the table.

Thankfully, Ethan spoke up. "Sorry about that, Mr. Shore. The roads were getting a bit dodgy with all the snow, and I wanted to be extra careful with Becca in the car."

Claire tilted her head in a silent "Aw," but her father remained unmoved. He stabbed his fork into the corn fritters, his attention completely fixed on Ethan. "So are you normally a reckless driver when my daughter's with you?"

Oh, shit! I can just see Daddy losing it when Ethan tells him about his motorcycle.

But Ethan remained unfazed by her father's accusation. "Not at all. In fact, I don't even own a car. Don't need one in the city."

"So you're subjecting her to riding in subways?"

Becca curled her fingers around her fork and bit back the snarky response that sat poised on her tongue. If her father hadn't cut her off, she wouldn't be riding in subways to begin with.

"If she wants to." Ethan dug into his fritter and finished chewing before continuing. "I've been known to spring for a cab when she doesn't."

His nonchalant handling of her father's interrogation amazed her, but she wondered how much longer he'd be able to keep it up. She'd seen him snap when pushed too far, and she didn't want that to happen here. "Ethan is every bit a gentleman," she told her father and prayed that would be the end of it.

But just to be safe, she sent a silent plea to her brother to help her out.

Jacob gave her the slightest of nods. "So, Ethan, how long have you been dating my sister?"

"Since around Rosh Hashanah." He turned to her, desire flaring in his eyes. "It's been a great two months."

Her cheeks grew warm, and she couldn't help but smile. "Agreed."

"You're Jewish?" Jacob continued.

"No, I'm not, but Becca was kind enough to invite me to dinner for the holiday and explain some of the customs to me."

Her father's nostrils flared, and he opened his mouth, but Claire cut him off before he could speak. "And what did you think of them?"

"They were sweet—literally and figuratively."

His joke made her uncle laugh, and the rest of the dinner guests eased into the meal.

Everyone, that was, except Becca and her father.

She kept her head low, her attention focused on her plate so she wouldn't make some gaffe at the table. While Claire directed the conversation around what Jacob and her cousins were doing, Becca's father continued to openly glare at Ethan like he was some gigolo who'd defiled his daughter.

They made it safely through the pear and walnut salad and the butternut squash bisque, but when the main course came out, Ethan pushed up the sleeves of his sweater to reveal his tattooed arms.

Her father's eyes bugged out. It was just the opportunity he was looking for to resume his interrogation. "So, Ethan, what do you do for a living?"

"I'm a musician," he replied before stuffing a forkful of turkey in his mouth.

Becca closed her eyes and prayed her father would stop, even though she knew better. Ethan's occupation had rekindled her father's opinion that she was nothing more than a fuck-up and added fuel to the fire.

"Musician, huh?" Her father arched one brow, his fork still hovering over his plate. "Isn't that just another term for 'unemployed'?"

"Daddy!" She'd had enough of this. "Will you just stop?"

Ethan placed his hand over hers, calming her. "It's okay, Bec. I'm used to people assuming that." Then he turned to her father. "I was in a band, but we broke up, and I'm pursuing a solo effort now."

"Which means you're between jobs." Her father sliced his meat with more force than necessary. "I bet you think you're lucky to have found my daughter."

"I'm thankful for every day I've known her," he replied, giving her a smile that made her insides turn to goo.

A Seductive Melody

Every female at the table appeared to be affected in a similar fashion, but her father continued to massacre his meal, his eyes never looking up from his plate. He gripped the knife like he wanted to stab someone, not cut the tender turkey breast.

"Yeah, I bet you are," her father grumbled. "But has she told you that she won't come into her trust fund until she's twenty-five? And even then, I might have the lawyers change her access to it so she doesn't blow it all on drugs."

Her appetite vanished, leaving behind a ball of fire that churned in the pit of her stomach. She was over being scared of her father. Now she was just plain pissed off. She dropped her knife and fork on her plate with a clatter, gaining her father's attention. "Daddy, that's enough."

"I'm only looking out for you, Becca. It's not like you have the best track record when it comes to making decisions."

"I know. You never let me forget I'm just like my mother." She tossed her napkin on her plate and stood up. "But as far as I'm concerned, the worst decision my mother ever made was marrying you."

The table fell silent, everyone watching the staring match between her and her father, waiting to see which one would yield first.

"Sit down, Rebecca, and quit making a scene," he ordered.

"I knew this was a mistake." She kicked her chair back and turned around. "I'm done."

She made for the front door as quickly as she could without running, never once looking over her shoulder to see if anyone followed. She'd tried to make amends with her father, but it was very clear that she'd never please him.

The quicker she could get back to Manhattan, the better.

***

Ethan observed Becca's mounting frustration all during the meal, so it was no surprise when she finally blew up. And this time, he didn't stop her. She needed to stand up to him, to say the things she said, if only to get them out of her system. Once she let go of the anger, it would be easier to move forward.

Her father regarded him with cold, narrowed eyes. "You'd better leave before she drives off without you."

"Doubt it." Ethan reached into his pocket and pulled out the keys.

"Then let me make this clear," Becca's father replied, his voice hard and even. "I know you're just after her money, and I'll do everything in my power to make sure you'll never see a cent of it."

"I'm perfectly fine with that, Mr. Shore." He crossed his arms and leaned back in his chair, a gesture to show that he wasn't going anywhere. "But just to clarify a few things—I don't need her money. I have plenty of my own."

He gulped back his hesitance and ignored the familiar tingle along his left arm. He was about to blow his cover for her. "Becca's been wonderful about keeping my identity under wraps, but in this instance, I feel it's necessary to tell you everything about me. My name is Ethan Kelly, and I was the lead singer of Ravinia's Rejects."

A Seductive Melody

"No way," her brother said, his eyes growing wider. "You guys are awesome."

"Thanks, man." He gave Jacob a grin before he turned back to her father. "As your son can tell you, we were doing pretty well before we lost our lead guitarist over the summer. Platinum records. World tours. Hell, the licensing alone for a fifteen second clip of one of our songs for a commercial was well into seven figures."

Her father's jaw slackened, but Ethan wasn't finished yet. If he was going to drop a bomb on her family, he might as well make sure it was enough to shake her father up.

"Furthermore, Mr. Shore, I have a trust fund of my own, not that I need it. My father was Sean Kelly of Kelly Properties in Chicago. I'm sure you've heard of him, too. He was the one who outbid you for that Michigan Avenue property a few years ago."

Becca's father remained statue still, the only perceptible movement being the subtle flare of his nostrils. He was a man who wasn't used to having his authority challenged, but Ethan wasn't ready to yield.

Now was the time to hammer the message home. "So you see, I'm not with Becca because of her money. I'm with her because of the amazing person she is. She was there for me when I was coming to grips with the loss of my bandmate and best friend and she helped me get my life back on track. And for that, I'll be eternally in her debt."

He stood up, slow and easy, still very much in control of the situation. "Everyone sees Becca as the person she was three years ago, and very few are ready to accept that she's grown and changed since then. They keep bringing up her past. But the thing is, we *all* make mistakes. It's what we learn from them that matters. I'm the one who convinced her to come today, and I hope I didn't make a mistake there.

"Now, if you'll excuse me, I'm going to check on her and see if I can convince her to come back to the table."

Ethan walked away to silence, but he held his head up a bit higher than usual. After months of hiding and doing everything he could to not be recognized, he'd finally come around to telling strangers who he was and taking credit for his accomplishments. It filled him with a sense of pride he hadn't had since the early days of his career.

But he'd have time to revel in that discovery later. Right now, he needed to find Becca and convince her to give her father one more chance. It was one thing to avoid personal demons. It was another to completely squash them. He'd learned that with his music and felt freer than ever. Now he needed to help Becca reach that same level of liberation.

He ran into Mrs. Cordero in the foyer. "Where's Becca?"

"Outside, by the woodpile." She handed Ethan his coat. "You're going to need this."

"Thanks." He slipped the coat on.

"You are most welcome." She reached up and pinched his cheek. "I knew I liked you."

He choked back a laugh. How many guests to the Shore home got a pinch from the housekeeper? But at least one person approved of him dating Becca.

The snow was coming down even harder than before,

blurring the world in white. Fat, heavy flakes accumulated on his shoulders, his hair, his eyelashes. A good two inches had fallen since they'd arrived, and with night approaching, returning to Manhattan was out of the question. They were stuck there for the night.

Slow, rhythmic *thunks* harmonized with feminine grunts on the other side of the house. He followed it until he found Becca chopping wood. She drove the blade of the ax into a log, splitting it within a few blows, and replaced it with a new log.

He came up behind her and grabbed the ax when she lifted it over her shoulder. "Trying to be a lumberjack?"

She let go of the handle and spun around. "You idiot. You could've been hurt."

"From this?" He held the ax like a guitar and pretended to play the blade.

He caught a hint of a smile on her face before she looked down and tried to pry the ax from his hands. "Give it back. I still need to work off some frustration."

"How about we dance with it?" He twisted the handle and twirled her around so she was pinned against him. The exercise had heightened the scent of her perfume, and he lowered his nose to the place behind her ear to breathe it in. He swayed his hips from side to side, guiding hers to match his movements in a slow foxtrot. "See? This is much nicer than chopping wood."

She stiffened and snatched the ax from him. "I need to split a few more logs."

He retreated out of range and leaned against the house with his hands in his pockets while she resumed chopping the wood. "You should come back inside. It's freezing out here."

"I'm staying plenty warm from this." She hefted the blade over her shoulder and brought it down with bone-chilling accuracy.

"But they'll be serving dessert soon."

She paused, and he hoped her love of sweets might entice her to return to her family. Then she shook her head. "Nope. If he's going to be a complete asshole, then I won't enjoy it."

"Too bad you didn't stick around. I think I might have convinced him I wasn't some loser looking for a piggy bank."

That made her stop. The ax fell from her hands as she turned to him. "What did you do?"

"I told him who I was." He came closer until his ice-cold nose was inches from her red one. "And I even threw in a little smackdown of my own thanks to a little tip from my brother."

"But I thought you didn't want people to know who you were."

"I don't, but in this case, I made an exception." He wrapped his arms around her and pulled her against him, tipping her head back so she looked up at him. "You're worth it."

Her face lit up just before he lowered his lips to hers. The kiss was slow and easy, but it didn't lack for passion. He grew harder with each passing second, and he was forced to end it before he was tempted to drag her to the nearest bed.

"Ethan, I—" She shivered and snuggled closer to him, tucking her head under his chin. "You're absolutely wonderful—do you know that?"

"You're pretty awesome yourself." *And I'm one lucky bastard to have you.* "So, how about dessert?"

She pulled back, her eyes clouded with doubt. "Maybe we can take it to go."

His shoulders slumped in defeat. He couldn't convince her to return to the table, but he still had all weekend to help her reconcile with her father. "Where?"

"That bungalow over there." She wriggled against him, sparking his desire in a way that demanded satisfaction. "I asked to stay there so you could fuck me as hard as you wanted, and no one would hear us."

His mouth went dry as all the blood rushed to his dick. "Why didn't you tell me that sooner?"

He tossed her over his shoulder and ran toward the cabin with Becca laughing the entire time.

***

Becca snuck into the kitchen and closed the back door as silently as she could behind her. The house was bathed in dark shadows and as silent as the falling snow outside. She'd dozed off after Ethan had made her come for the fourth time that evening, but her growling stomach reminded her that she'd missed out on most of Thanksgiving dinner. She was tiptoeing toward the fridge to find some leftovers when the lights came on.

Her heart jumped. She froze and dared to peek over her shoulder at the person who'd caught her.

"Can't sleep either?" Claire asked. She wrapped her dressing gown around her nightie and tied it closed as she came closer. Even after having Jacob, she'd retained her ready-for-the-runway figure that had helped her grace dozens of magazine covers in the late eighties and early nineties.

"Just hungry." She opened the fridge and grabbed the container of turkey, followed by the bag of bread. "Can I make you anything?"

"No, but I'll have a few sips of milk." She sat down on one of the stools surrounding the giant island in the center of the kitchen.

"Coming right up." She added the milk carton to her pile and made her way to the other side of the island. She poured a glass for her stepmother. "Sorry about dinner, Claire. I tried. I really did."

"I know, dear, but you know your father." She gave a weary sigh and stared at her milk, not touching it. "I give kudos to Ethan for standing up to him like he did. None of your previous boyfriends had the gumption to do that."

Becca smiled as she fixed her sandwich. "Yeah, he's a great guy."

"I didn't know he was famous until he told us, but once your brother pulled him up on the Internet, I recognized him." She took a sip of milk. "He looks better with the short hair."

Becca found herself giggling. "He's pretty sexy, all right. But he's more than a hot bod with a dreamy voice. He makes me feel like a million bucks when I'm around him."

"How did you two meet?"

She hesitated, wondering how Claire would react if she knew the whole truth. "We, um, met at one of my NA meetings."

Her stepmother raised both brows. "He's a recovering

addict like you?"

Becca nodded, finishing her sandwich and starting on another one for Ethan. "His best friend died of an overdose, and he took that as a sign he needed to get clean before he ended up the same way."

"But isn't that dangerous? Aren't you worried he'll relapse and tempt you to do the same?"

"Not at all." She layered slice after slice of turkey on the bread, followed by a leaf of lettuce. "I'm so proud of how far he's come. And we're good about supporting each other to avoid that temptation to relapse." She paused, remembering something he'd said to her months ago. "He gets me."

"I understand that, Becca, but I'm still worried."

"Don't be." She shook the milk carton. There was enough left for her and Ethan to each have a glass. She tucked it under her arm and grabbed the plate with the sandwiches on it. "Seriously, Claire, you have no idea how good he's been for me. And every time I'm around him, I find myself discovering one more reason to fall in love with him."

She started for the door, but Claire dashed in front of her and cut her off. Her stepmother wrapped her arms around her in a hug. "I'm glad to hear that, Becca, but please, don't run off and elope without first letting me know."

Becca laughed. "We've only been dating two months, Claire. Marriage is way off in the distance."

"But sometimes you just know." She twirled the wedding band around her own finger. "Your father and I had only been dating that long when he proposed."

Yeah, and I still don't see how someone as wonderful as you has stayed married as long as you have to someone like my father.

She gave her stepmother a tight smile. "Like I said, we're in no hurry."

But as she made her way back to the bungalow, she found herself wondering what it would be like to be married to Ethan Kelly.

Chapter Thirteen

Ethan pressed one side of the headphones against his ear and grooved along with the song. "This is fuckin' awesome," he told his sound engineer, Damian.

"Thanks, man." He gave Ethan a fist bump. "But seriously, dude, those are some killer sweet tracks you laid down. Made it easy to mix them into that."

The song ended, but the grin on his face didn't fade. The new album was different from anything he'd ever recorded. For the first time in his career, he didn't have a record label telling him to stick with the hard rock sound that had made Ravinia's Rejects famous. The rock influences were still there, but he'd mixed in blues and country and electronic beats, depending on the different songs. The result was a compilation that was uniquely him.

And he liked it.

Up until this point, he'd been plagued by fear, doubt, and the ever-persistent cravings. Many nights, he left the studio wondering what he'd gotten himself into. He questioned his talent, his vision, even his sanity. His old muse beckoned him to return, but he fought back by holding on to his newfound freedom and the joy of making music that wasn't tainted by heroin. As Becca told him months ago, the cravings never completely went away, but they became easier to deal with.

Today, however, was the first day he could listen to his music and not associate it with the past.

He put down the headphones and pointed to the thumb drive on Damian's laptop. "Can I take that home to show my girlfriend?"

"It's all yours." Damian made a few clicks on the keyboard and popped the drive out. "Let me know if you need me to tweak anything else."

"Will do. And remember, this needs to stay under wraps until I drop the news."

"No problem, man. I'm cool like that." He started packing up his gear. "And any time you want to work together, I'm game."

"Right on." He tucked the USB drive in his pocket and grabbed his jacket. He couldn't wait to see what Becca thought of it. "Talk to you soon."

Ethan got on his motorcycle and zoomed out of the parking garage under the recording studio. The early December air had a definite bite to it as he rode from Hell's Kitchen to Midtown, but the bright lights and holiday decorations chased away the dreariness of the long nights.

That, and the constant presence of a certain warm body in his bed every night.

He pulled in front of the building where Becca worked and he parked his bike, waiting for the moment where she'd emerge from the revolving door. He didn't have to wait long.

A Seductive Melody

Becca came running out of the lobby wearing leggings that clung to every delicious line of her legs. She blew him a kiss before putting on her helmet and climbing behind him. "Right on time."

"Wouldn't want to keep you waiting." He revved the engine up and ventured north toward Central Park.

It was Friday afternoon, and he had a fun date planned for the two of them. After a string of high-society events over the last two months, he was looking forward to the opportunity to just be a regular person. As he got closer to the park, he slowed down until he found a place to safely park his bike.

"What are we doing?" she asked.

"It's a surprise." He helped her off his bike and secured the helmet. "Just come with me."

They strolled through the park arm in arm, talking about their day, but he didn't tell her about the finished album. The USB drive in his pocket reminded him he still had one more surprise for her after this.

Her eyes lit up in delight when they turned the corner and she saw the Wollman ice skating rink. "Is this what we're doing?"

"Yeah." He guided her to the front of the line and pulled out the two advance tickets he'd purchased earlier that week. "I figured Rockefeller would be a little too touristy, but I still wanted to do something to get us in the holiday mood."

"You do realize that Hanukkah is a minor holiday and still a week and a half away?" she teased before giving her shoe size to the clerk at the skate rental stand.

"I know, and Christmas is even further off, but I don't

care. I wanted to experience the excitement, the thrill of being a kid again and marveling at the twinkling lights." He handed her the rental skates. "Humor me."

She playfully rolled her eyes, her grin defying any hint of sarcasm. "I guess I will."

The skates weren't like the hockey blades he'd learned to skate on as a child, and when he got onto the ice, he stumbled forward. His arms flailed out in an attempt to catch his balance, smacking Becca in the chest. A sick feeling formed in the pit of his gut, but he couldn't tell if it was from accidentally hitting her or from making a fool of himself in front of everyone.

Becca's laughter eased his nerves. She took his hand and led him around the ice. "First time skating?"

"Please. My older brother's an NHL goalie. We all spent time on the ice growing up." He pointed to the jagged tip on the blades. "Of course, hockey skates don't have these on them."

"It's called a toe pick."

"Whatever." The toe pick caught the ice again, pitching him forward. "Motherfucker!"

Maybe this wasn't such a great idea after all.

"You're doing it wrong," Becca said, still laughing. "It's meant to be used like this."

She let go of his hand and glided out toward the center of the ice, picking up speed as she skated. Then she planted the pick into the ice and jumped. Two revolutions later, she landed on one blade and moved into a fast spin, her elegant arms reaching up into the sky.

He watched her, his chest swelling up with pride. She was beautiful, and he still couldn't believe she was his.

When she skated back to him, he gave her a lighthearted bump with his shoulder. "Show-off."

"Hey, five years of skating lessons paid off." She took his hand again. "Are you ready for your lesson, Mr. Kelly?"

"No, I'd rather circle the rink a few times with a gorgeous woman by my side."

Her cheeks turned pink. "I work at a magazine. I'm sure we could secure a model for you."

"I don't need a model, not when I have you." He brushed his lips against her forehead.

Her blush deepened, and she bit her bottom lip.

God, does she have any idea how much that turns me on? The blood rushed straight to his dick, and he resisted the urge to suck that lip between his own teeth in a kiss that would make the parents at the rink cover their children's eyes.

She pushed off with her skates, moving them back into the rink's traffic. "So, what were holidays like with your family?"

"Chaos." But as he shared stories from his childhood, he grew nostalgic for the times he'd shared with his brothers. Caleb and Frank were usually the ringleaders when it came to getting them in trouble, but Adam was always the one who kept them from burning the house down or getting arrested. In the end, he wouldn't trade any of those memories.

He grew quiet and looked down at Becca. A thoughtful smile lingered on her lips, and her distant gaze was far beyond the rink. "What are you thinking?" he asked.

"That your experience was so different than mine."

If Thanksgiving was any indication, he could only

imagine how stiff and formal her holidays must have been. "No food fights over the dinner table or stuffing your face full of chocolate?"

She shook her head. "Jacob is four years younger than me and could've gotten away with it, but my father kept me on a tight leash. I was even limited to only one piece of chocolate gelt a night during Hanukkah. But Claire would always slip me a few more when he wasn't looking."

"Are you planning on celebrating Hanukkah with them this year?"

She drew in a sharp breath, her entire body tightening. "Not likely."

He skated halfway around the rink, gathering up his courage before offering to bring her into his insanity. "Would you consider coming home with me for Christmas?"

She pulled him out the traffic and spun around in front of him. "You're inviting me to meet your family?"

"Don't act so surprised. You took me to meet yours." He cradled her face in his hands, his heart pumping full of an emotion he still was frightened to acknowledge. How could he have fallen in love with her so quickly? And yet as he stared into her bright blue-green eyes, he couldn't imagine not loving her. "I promise to protect you from Jasper. And Frank."

She leaned forward, perfectly balanced on those damn toe picks, and kissed him. "I may have to consider your offer."

"What is there to consider?"

"Meeting your mom, for starters." She slipped back to his side and merged them back into the throng of skaters, her gaze fixed on the ice. "I know I don't have the best reputation."

Guilt nagged at him. Her reputation was one of the reasons why he hadn't told anyone in his family he was dating her. They would jump to the worst conclusions based on her past behavior. "Maybe, but you've changed. Besides, we don't have to tell them until they get to know you first and see how far you've come from your former life."

"Do you really think they'd be able to?"

"Absolutely," he said, full of false confidence. Of course, Adam would probably order a background check on her, and her mother would pick her apart like the prosecuting attorney she'd once been. But once they got to know her, they'd see all the wonderful things he did.

He squeezed her hand. "They'll love you."

Almost as much as I do.

***

Becca made revolution after revolution around the rink with Ethan, still mulling over his request. He wanted her to meet his family. And if his mother was anything like her prior boyfriends' moms, she'd instantly assume Becca wasn't good enough for her son and go about proving it. All it would take was one Google search to bring up the mistakes of her past as evidence.

Of course, it was the next step in a relationship—meeting the other family. Most girls would be thrilled at the idea of having Ethan Kelly take them home to meet his mother, but all she knew was fear. She was falling in love with him. Her estrangement from her father made his disapproval of their relationship easy to ignore, but would

Ethan be able to do the same if his family hated her?

Ethan remained silent for several minutes before saying, "Sorry to spring that on you, Bec. I just thought—"

She shushed him with her finger. "It's fine. I'm more nervous than anything else, that's all."

"Don't be." He pulled her into his arms, tucking her hand under his beside the place where his heart beat. "If my brother can introduce his pregnant girlfriend to my mom over Thanksgiving and not land in deep shit, I can definitely bring you." He paused, his brows drawing together. "Unless you're knocked up and haven't told me yet."

"Oh, good grief!" She tried to wriggle out of his arms, but he held on tighter, laughing the entire time. "Don't even joke about that."

"Just trying to show you that you have nothing to worry about." He placed a quick peck on her lips and let go.

As she spun around, a camera flash caught her eye. Normally, she'd expect families to snap photos of their kids on the ice, but she couldn't shake the chill that crept up her spine from it. She searched the crowd for its source and spied a man holding a camera with a massive zoom lens pointed right at her and Ethan.

"I think we've been spotted." She gave a discreet nod toward the photographer as they continued to skate, noting how he followed their every move.

Ethan watched him out of the corner of his eye, his jaw clenching.

"Want to leave?" she asked.

A Seductive Melody

"Yeah." He led her to a bench and yanked off his skates. "I fuckin' hate the paparazzi."

"Who likes them?" But the tingle along her spine wouldn't ebb. There was something familiar about that photographer. She'd seen him before, but for the life of her, she couldn't remember where. Her younger years had been a blur of camera flashes, so it wouldn't be too much to assume she'd seen him then.

Ethan turned in her skates and herded her away from the rink. "Here's to hoping we can lose him in the park."

They made it back to his bike without any more camera flashes. Ethan remained tense and silent as he handed her helmet to her, every inch of him hyper-vigilant as though he was expecting a knife-wielding stalker to rush at them at any moment.

"It's just a photographer," she said in an attempt to calm him down.

"I know, but I also know how dangerous they can be when they're pursuing their targets." He strapped his helmet on. "I don't want you to get hurt."

But as they rode back to his place, Becca couldn't help but feel that part of their fairytale romance was coming to an end. It was one thing to just be a normal couple. But when fame entered the equation, it added a whole new level of complications.

"I'm sorry our date had to end on a sour note," she said once they reached his loft.

"I'm not." He propped his motorcycle up in its usual spot and hung his jacket on the hooks next to the helmets. "Besides, it gives me a chance to show you this."

He pulled a thumb drive out of his pocket and plugged

it into his laptop.

She peered over his shoulder as he entered in a password to access its contents. "Top secret information you stole from the Russians?"

He chuckled and handed her a pair of Bluetooth headphones. "Not quite."

She put them on and was immersed in a world of music. Sweet, yet dark and haunting, it made her pulse quicken even while her hips swayed to the beat. Her breath caught as she listened to the familiar voice sing of finding himself in the darkness and coming back into the light. Unshed tears burned her eyes, and she covered her mouth to keep from blubbering like a baby. She'd always loved Ravinia's Rejects, but Ethan had taken the music to a deeper, more personal level that tugged on her heart and took her on the journey with him.

Ethan hung on her every reaction until the song ended, his eyes lit up with expectation. Sarcasm dripped from his voice as he asked, "It sucked, didn't it?"

Laughter overtook her tears, and she playfully punched him in the chest. "Oh yeah, it totally sucked."

He wrapped his arms around her waist and pulled her to him. "Tell me what you really think, Bec."

"It's fuckin' brilliant, just like you." She threaded her fingers through his hair and lowered his lips to hers.

"So you like it?"

"Yes, I do."

"And do I get a thank-you for letting you be the first person to listen to it?" He grabbed her ass, the hard ridge of his erection pressing to the lower part of her stomach and heating the desire in her own blood.

A Seductive Melody

"I'm sure I can think of something."

"So can I."

He lifted her up, and her legs instinctively wrapped around his waist. One passionate kiss led to another, each more hungry than the last, until he carried her up to his bed and left her completely sated.

Chapter Fourteen

Hilde was waiting at Becca's cubicle when she arrived at work Monday morning. The weekend had been a blissful haze of passionate lovemaking and music as Ethan slowly unveiled one song at a time to her, but all that came to an end when her alarm bleated that morning.

"I got your text message." Becca handed Hilde her coffee. "Anything else?"

"Elaine was looking for you."

Becca glanced at the clock and cursed. She was almost half an hour late. "Was she pissed?"

"When isn't she?" Hilde took a sip from her cup before continuing. "She made me wait here until you showed up so I could relay her message to you."

"Which was?"

"She wants to see you in her office. Pronto." Hilde walked off, drinking her coffee as though there was nothing amiss.

Cold sweat prickled the base of Becca's spine. Even if Elaine had good news for her, she was not at her desk when she was supposed to be. She stowed her bag, wiped her palms on her skirt, and made her way to the editor's corner office.

Elaine's secretary gave her a tight smile. "She's been expecting you, Rebecca."

Shit! Not a good sign when the secretary is on alert. Is it too early to start asking for boxes for my things?

She paused at the door, took a deep breath to collect herself, and knocked.

"Come in," Elaine called from the other side.

Becca swallowed past the lump in her throat and entered. "You asked to see me, Elaine?"

The editor stood at her desk, focused on the papers scattered around it. "Yes, I did. Come here."

As she approached the desk, her fear multiplied into horror. The papers Elaine was studying were pictures of her and Ethan. Walking through Hell's Kitchen. At the Wollman rink. At the river. At Gitta's café. Even of them skiing in the Catskills during Thanksgiving weekend.

Elaine looked up, her sharp eyes boring holes into her. "You've been holding out on me."

Becca tried to speak, but her throat tightened, strangling her.

"I asked you to give me celebrity dirt, and all this time, you've been sitting on the story of a lifetime." She held up a picture of Becca kissing Ethan.

Her voice shook as she asked, "You've been spying on me?"

"Of course." She dropped the photograph and went back to her chair. "When your father mentioned that you'd brought Ethan Kelly home for Thanksgiving dinner—"

"My father told you we were dating?" She knew he

didn't like Ethan, but this took it to a whole other level.

"Don't interrupt." Elaine's words were sharper than a samurai's katana. "And yes, I had lunch with your parents last week, and they told me all about your new boyfriend. I wouldn't have believed them, but they showed me these pictures." She tapped the ones of them skiing.

"I knew what a huge story this would be, so I sent Armando to follow you." She waved her hand over the rest of the photographs. "You've been a very busy girl."

Becca sank into the chair across from Elaine, regretting the bagel she'd downed for breakfast that now churned in her stomach like the Hudson in a nor'easter. "What do you want, Elaine?"

"You've been asking to write a story, and now I'm giving you your very own assignment." The editor steepled her fingers and sat back in her chair. "I want a tell-all exclusive. Ethan Kelly is an enigma, and since the death of his bandmate, he's gone even further underground. Yet you seem to know him quite intimately."

The answer formed on her lips before she even had a chance to think about it. "No."

"Journalism is all about the big story, the one that will captivate the public and sell newspapers and magazines and bring clicks to websites. And I'm sure thousands of women would eagerly buy a copy of *Moderne* if it contained an exposé of Ethan Kelly. I want details of his battle with addiction, of his new album, of his reaction to his bandmate's death."

"I won't do that to him."

Elaine made a *tsk*ing sound with her tongue. "And that's why you'll never succeed at journalism. It can never be personal. It's always business. You can't let your emotions interfere with the story."

She winced at the coldness of Elaine's comments. If that was what it meant to be a true journalist, she wanted none of it. "But he's my boyfriend, not some stranger on the street."

"He's a public figure readers want to know more about." Elaine leaned forward on her desk, her expression turning into one of impatient tolerance. "Rebecca, dear, the only reason I've kept you here as long as I have is because I'm good friends with your parents. When your father mentioned to me that you wanted to become a serious journalist, I nearly laughed my head off. But since he asked me to help you out, I agreed to offer you a job. So far, you've lived up to my expectations."

Judging from the way Elaine looked down her nose at her, those expectations weren't set very high to begin with.

But the sting of Elaine's assessment was nothing compared the harsh humiliation of the truth. The only reason she was there was because of her father. It didn't matter that she'd worked her tail off to graduate from NYU's Journalism Institute. To the entire world, she would always be Becca Shore, heiress and fucked-up party girl.

"I'm giving you a chance to prove me wrong, Rebecca." She held up a photograph from the ice rink. "I want a story on Ethan Kelly in my in-box by Friday afternoon. If you can't do it, then don't bother returning to work on Monday."

She dropped the picture and shooed Becca away. "You have your assignment. Don't disappoint me."

Becca's knees shook as she rose from the chair, but she forced herself to leave in a calm, controlled manner. Somehow, she made it out of the corner office without losing it. The nausea refused to relent, though, and she wound up making a dash to the nearest bathroom to lose her breakfast. Hot tears followed, and she hugged the toilet while her frustration vented.

She needed this job. If she lost it, she'd be forced to become dependent on someone else again, and every fiber of her being recoiled at that idea. But her conscience refused to allow her to keep her job by betraying the man she loved.

There has to be some middle ground. There must be.

Her tears dried up, and she turned her energy to finding it.

***

Ethan stared at the timeline on the white board in front of him, the end of a dry erase marker pressed against the corner of his mouth. In the past, he'd always let someone at his record label handle the details of a new release. Now, he was in charge.

The hard part was over. He'd finished an album he was proud of in record time. But a whole new realm of unfamiliar territory loomed in front of him. When should he announce the new solo album? How? Website? Press release? Should he slip a sample to a local radio station?

And of course, once he went public with the news, the simple life he'd enjoyed while hiding would come to an end. He'd have to make appearances on TV shows and at concerts. People would recognize him on the streets after that, and he'd be faced with more instances like Friday night.

The inside of his wrist burned, flowing up to the back of his neck. A cold sweat prickled his skin. His muscles clenched, and his gut wrenched. The craving blindsided him with enough force to make him stumble back in his chair. Several minutes passed as he concentrated on the air moving in and out of his lungs, thankful for each breath that he drew in. He could beat this, just like he'd had dozens of times before. He just had to remind himself all the other things that filled the void.

A few minutes later, the craving passed, and the world came back into focus. He turned to his computer and did a quick Internet search for his name. No new pictures came up. Whoever the paparazzo was, he hadn't sold those pictures of him and Becca at the ice rink to any media outlet.

His phone rang, and he answered without looking at the number.

"Hello, sweetie," his mom said in a honey-thick voice. "How are you doing?"

"I'd be doing a lot better if you'd stop talking to me like I was still five years old, Mom." He tried to sound stern, but a hint of teasing crept into his words. "Yes, I'm fine. No, I haven't used any drugs. And yes, I'm back to work. Any other questions?"

"Where did you learn how to be such a smartass?"

Laughter broke free from his chest. "Frank," he replied.

"I'll have to talk to that boy when he comes home for Christmas. Speaking of which..."

He set the marker on the table and hopped up on the

kitchen counter. "I'm coming home, Mom. Don't worry about that."

"Wonderful! I'll get to have all of my boys home at once. We haven't been able to do that for three years."

"It's not my fault Ben and Frank always have games around the holidays, or that Caleb's always getting deployed somewhere."

"Or that you were always on the road with the band."

"Well, I am kind of busy arranging the release of my first solo effort, but I suppose I can put it off until after the holidays." He closed his eyes and smiled, enjoying the freedom of controlling his career. It meant he could enjoy a peaceful holiday without dozens of reporters hounding his every move. "Is Dan bringing his girlfriend?"

"Yes, even though poor little Jenny's going to be massively pregnant by then. Why?"

The peace from moments before was slowly eroded by nerves. "Um, would it be okay if I bring my girlfriend, too?"

He could almost picture his mom's mouth hanging agape during the silence that followed. "You have a girlfriend and you didn't tell me?"

"Mom, I'm an adult now, remember? I don't have to tell you every little detail of my life."

"But you should at least tell me if you're seeing someone."

"Not if it's still early in the relationship. I wanted to make sure she was a keeper before telling anyone."

"Exactly how long have you been dating her?"

He ran his finger along the neck band of his T-shirt. "About three months. Nowhere near proposal time, Mom, so don't even bring that up."

"Fine, I won't." Although the exasperated tone revealed her disappointment.

"And don't go overly religious with the decorations. She's Jewish."

"Jewish?"

"I think that's enough information for now, Mom. Just don't overwhelm her when you meet her, okay?"

"Can I at least have her name?"

"Becca." He hung up before his mom could pry any more information from him. Becca was already nervous enough about her past being a strike against her, and he didn't want to give his mom anything that could make her more uncomfortable. She'd respected his identity when it came to meeting her family, and he could do the same for her.

Besides, they were bound to like her. And once they got to know the real Becca, then he could mention her last name.

He went back to the white board and continued planning his release, scouting out PR firms until his alarm went off to remind him of his weekly NA meeting. He grabbed his helmet and jacket and wondered what specials Gitta would have this week at her café.

***

Ari did a double take when she came into the apartment. "What are you doing home this early, Becca? Don't you have your meeting to go to?"

Becca curled her knees up to her chest, already dressed in her pajamas on the sofa. "I got sick at work."

Panic flickered over her roommate's face. "Stay away

from me. I can't afford to get sick right now. I have a project due before I leave for LA next week."

"It's not that kind of sick."

Panic change to concern. "Uh-oh. You're not pregnant, are you?"

"What the fuck is up with all the pregnancy concerns?" She tossed a pillow at her roommate. "I've been taking my pill every day at the same time like I should, thank you very much."

"Sorry, but you seem a little, um, *emotional* lately." Ari lowered her bottom to the edge of the chair and folded her hands in her lap. "What's wrong?"

"Where do I start?"

"Wherever you want. I'm still your best friend, after all."

For the first time since her meeting with Elaine that morning, she didn't feel sick to her stomach. "I mentioned to you that I thought I saw someone taking pictures of me and Ethan at the ice rink Friday. Well, I found out why. Elaine hired him to track me. She has photos of the two of us all over the city."

Ari's lips parted in surprise, and her brown eyes grew to twice their normal size. "That fucking bitch."

"Oh, you don't know the half of it. She asked me to write an exposé on Ethan. Told me if I didn't turn it in by Friday, I was as good as fired."

"Oh my god! The nerve of that woman."

"And the kicker was that the only reason she hired me was because Daddy called in a favor." Becca grabbed another pillow and hugged it to her chest. "So now I'm faced with either betraying Ethan or losing the job I only have because of my father."

"This calls for wine." Ari rose from her chair and disappeared into the kitchen. She returned a minute later with a bottle of red wine, a corkscrew, and two glasses.

"You know I don't drink."

"Yes, but if there was ever a reason to let your rules slide, this is it." She poured two glasses and handed one to Becca. "So, let's brainstorm our options."

Becca held her glass, refusing to sip from it, but gave her roommate a smile. This was what she loved about Ari. Growing up, she'd always found a way to get around rules and restrictions, and Becca hoped her best friend would help her find a way around this.

Ari took a generous drink from her glass. "Okay, let's start with the extremes. Option one: You tell Elaine to take this job and shove it."

Becca snorted with laughter as she imagined the editor's face reacting to that statement. She set her glass down before she spilled the contents. "I so do not have the balls for that."

"You used to." Ari took another drink. "Option two: You beg your boyfriend for the story to save your job."

She squirmed at the thought of that. "I don't know, Ari. Ethan's very private, and the kind of things Elaine wants—well, I hate to ask that of him."

Ari gave her a sympathetic nod. "But if you at least explained your situation to him—"

"No, I can't." Becca threw down her pillow and paced in front of the sofa. "After all, I'm the reason the paparazzi found us. If I hadn't taken him home for Thanksgiving, then my dad wouldn't have told Elaine about him, and there wouldn't be any photographs out there of him. Don't you see—his privacy is being threatened, and it's all my fault."

"Maybe, but it's not like you sold him out. After all, he was the one who wanted to come home with you. He's the one who told your father who he was."

"I know, but..." She stopped and pressed her palm to her forehead. No matter how hard she tried to rationalize everything, she still felt like a failure. "I tried so hard to protect him."

"But he's a big boy, Becca. He can take care of himself now."

"Is he? To me, he's still fragile, still in danger of one blow setting him back on the wrong path again."

"And you're not?" Ari stood and came next to her. "Let's say you do what you consider the ethical thing and quietly refuse to write the story. You'll lose the only job you've ever had, and the market right now isn't hopping with new ones. As soon as you give your name, people are going to draw their own conclusions about you. We have this place rent-free, but I can only cover so much of the food and utilities."

"You don't think I haven't considered that?"

"So then you're faced with two other options. One: go crawling back to your father and beg for a monthly allowance."

Becca wrinkled her nose, every fiber of her being repulsed at the idea. "You know I won't do that."

"The other option is that you make Ethan your sugar daddy and move in with him. He certainly has the funds to support you, and you're practically living there anyway."

A Seductive Melody

"I'd still be a leech." She sank back down on the sofa. "The whole idea behind this journalism thing was to be independent, to not have to rely on someone else's money to get by."

"Yeah, but people like you and me are always going to have to prove that we're something more than spoiled little rich girls."

"You seem to have no trouble with your job."

"That's because I'm doing something I love. Press releases, social events, media spotlights—they're all right up my alley."

Elaine's statements about not letting her emotions interfere with her stories came back to haunt her. "I thought I felt the same way about journalism."

Ari sat down next to her and gave her a hug. "Don't give up on it, yet. You'll find a way to do what you love."

The doorbell rang, and Ari got up to answer it.

Ethan's voice came in from the doorway. "Ari, Becca wasn't at the meeting—"

She looked up from the sofa, not caring that she was wearing old flannel PJs and sporting a pair of red-rimmed eyes from crying.

Ethan crossed the room in less than a dozen long-legged strides and crouched down in front of her. "Are you okay?"

She forced a weak smile on her face for him. "I will be."

"When you weren't at the meeting, I got worried."

Her heart flopped, reminding her of all the reasons why she'd never betray him. "I went home sick from work, that's all."

"Would this cheer you up?" He pulled a small box bearing the logo from Gitta's café. "She said it was some kind of holiday cake and that you would like it."

She stroked his cheek. "Thank you, Ethan. That was very sweet of you."

His eye flickered over to the glass of wine beside her, and his lips pressed together. "Is there anything else I can do for you?"

Ari stood behind Ethan, signaling that she should tell him about the situation, but Becca just shook her head. "I just need some time to mend."

He glanced once more at the wine glass before rising. "Give me a call if you need anything."

He leaned over to place a kiss on her forehead and said good-bye to Ari before letting himself out.

Her roommate jumped right into the place he'd vacated in front of her. "What is wrong with you, Becca? He wants to help, and you just pushed him away."

"I can get through this without him."

"Bullshit." Ari took a step back. "You know trust is essential to a good relationship."

"Yes, and he's entrusted me with his secrets, and I'm not going to exploit them to save my career."

"But trust is a two-way street, Becca. You have to trust him, too."

"I—" She couldn't come up with a good excuse. Ari was right. She needed to trust Ethan with her secrets, too. But she hated the thought of dumping her problems on him. "I'll sleep on it."

"Fine, but I hope you get over your reservations, or it's going to become a big problem between you two."

Becca retreated to her bedroom and tried to go to sleep, but no matter what she did, she couldn't quiet her troubled mind. There simply was no easy way out of her predicament. She tossed and turned well after she heard her roommate go to bed and finally got up a little after one. A few seconds later, she was dialing Ethan's number.

"You up?" he asked when he answered.

"Yeah. You?"

"Yeah."

Her voice sounded small and meek as she asked, "Is it too late for me to come over?"

"Do you want me to come and get you?"

"No, I can get a cab." She checked her wallet to make sure she'd have enough cash for the fare. "I'll be there in a bit."

She threw on some clothes and hailed a taxi.

Ethan was waiting for her when she arrived and pulled her into his arms. "What's wrong, Bec?"

"You know that expression, 'Between a rock and a hard place'? Well, try smashed between the boulder and cliff face."

He tightened his arms around her and led her up the stairs. "Care to explain it to me?"

"Maybe." She shook off her jacket and shoes and crawled into bed next to him, her body instinctively curling along his. "It's a work issue."

"Tell me about it." He massaged her scalp while he waited.

Her eyes grew heavy from the fatigue of the day, and she risked falling asleep if she didn't unburden her soul soon. "My editor gave me an assignment I disagree with."

"Why?"

She chewed her bottom lip, wondering how much she should reveal to him. "Because people could get hurt if I write it."

"And if you don't?"

"I'm fired."

He sucked in a breath through his teeth. "Tough call."

"Now you know why I'm torn."

"Yeah, but I also know you. You'll listen to your heart and do the right thing."

"Even if it means the end of my journalism career?"

"Who says it's the end? You're a brilliant woman, Bec, and it won't take you long to find another job, even if it's freelance writing." He gave her a playful jostle. "Besides, didn't you say you hated working there anyway?"

"I do." She snuggled closer to him, the worries of the day finally slipping away. Ethan believed in her. Now she just had to believe in herself and do the right thing. "Thank you for making me feel better."

"Any time." He planted a gentle kiss on the top of her head and held her until she fell asleep.

Chapter Fifteen

Becca strolled into her father's office Thursday morning, ignoring the protests of his secretary. Two days had passed without a solution to her work problem, but she could at least deal with her father. "Daddy, we need to talk."

He looked up from his computer screen, one brow arched above his cool blue-green eyes, and dismissed his secretary. "Have a seat, Rebecca."

She took the chair across from him and crossed her legs, her spine ramrod straight with determination. "First off, I don't appreciate you telling Elaine about Ethan."

"We were merely having lunch as old friends, and the conversation turned to you."

"Yes, but now she's forcing me to write a story about his personal life or I risk losing my job. A job, I found out, that I only have because of you."

"You were running into dead ends with this ridiculous pursuit of a journalism career, and I opened a door for you."

"But it's not ridiculous to me. This is what I want to do with my life."

"Oh, please. You can't stay clean long enough to hold down a responsible job. And dating another addict like that rock star is only going to drag you down further."

She jumped to her feet, her skin burning with rage. "First off, I've been clean for almost three years, and it stopped being an issue once I cut myself free from your controlling and manipulating ways. Second, Ethan is a recovering addict, just like me. We help each other stay clean."

"Or you can pull each other back into that cesspool of heroin, just like what happened to your mother."

She drew in a deep breath before she launched a series of four-lettered words at her father. "I have no memory of my mother, so I can't say if I'm like her or not. But I do know that the reason I started using was because of you."

Surprise flickered across his face, shocking the muscles lax for a brief second before the controlled mask of composure settled back into place. "Don't try to point the finger at me. We both know that addiction has a genetic component."

"Maybe, but the way you always demanded perfection from me didn't help. Do you have any idea how fucking great it was to not care what you thought of me? To be comfortable in my own skin without being reminded of the hundreds of things you found wrong with me?"

He settled back in his chair, his fingers splayed against his mouth in a pensive gesture.

"I know I've always been a disappointment to you. I know you don't expect me to be much more than some loser addict with a trust fund. But you're wrong. I found something I wanted to do. I wanted to tell stories that invoked change. I wanted to champion the wronged and make others aware of the difficult situations all around us. I wanted to write articles that would eventually make someone's life better. And no one believed in me except for Ari."

She pressed her hands against the immaculate glass top of his desk and leaned forward. "I know why you told Elaine about me and Ethan, and I'm here to tell you that although your stunt may end up costing me my job, I'm not giving up on my dream, and I'm not giving him up, either."

She turned around on her high heels and left without another word.

After spending the last three days feeling like her world was crumbling, she finally felt like she was back in control. Telling her father off got one monkey off her back, and by the time she reached the ground-floor lobby of his office tower, she had an idea about what to do with Elaine.

***

Ethan played a few notes on his piano and wrote them down with a grin. Even though he was still trying to set up the release of a new album, the music kept coming. At the rate he was going, he'd have another album's worth of material ready to record by spring.

He only wished things could be this easy for Becca. The last couple of nights, she'd tossed and turned beside him, only sleeping after he made love to her in the wee hours of the morning. She hadn't gone back to her office, choosing to chew up half a dozen of his pencils while she scribbled idea after idea only to toss her notes into the shredder a few minutes later. This morning was the first time she'd woken up with a determined look in her eye and it gave him hope that she'd found a solution to her problem.

She left before dawn to go back to her apartment, and he hadn't heard from her since then. He hoped that her silence was a good sign.

He worked out a few more bars of music before his phone rang with her number on the display. "Hey, beautiful, how you doing?"

"Much better. I turned in a story to Elaine, and I'm looking at flights to the Caribbean. There's one leaving for Barbados tomorrow morning at six. Want to make a quick little getaway with me?"

He glanced outside at the snow piling up on his windowsill. "Some sunshine and warm sand sound great to me."

"Awesome. Booking the flight right now. It leaves out of JFK, so why don't we meet at my place before heading over there?"

"Done." He ended the call with a bigger grin than before. Becca was back to her usual fearless self, and he couldn't wait to see what kind of fun they could have in the tropics. It was just the sort of vacation he needed before he put himself back in the public spotlight again.

And it would provide the perfect opportunity to convince her to come home with him for Christmas.

***

Becca's knee wouldn't stop twitching as the plane zoomed down the runway for takeoff. *What was I thinking, getting on a plane? I hate flying.* But it was a spur of the moment thing. She needed to get away, and Claire had been kind enough to slip her a credit card number for emergencies months ago.

And turning in a story that would probably cost her the only job she'd ever had counted as an emergency.

Ethan steadied her by placing his hand on her thigh. "Should I ask the flight attendant for a barf bag?"

She shook her head. "First time I've flown in a while, that's all."

She didn't have to add it was the first time she'd flown sober. Ethan nodded, the understanding in his gray eyes telling her he understood exactly what she meant. "At least it's first class."

"Yeah, it's a bit of a splurge." She looked out the window at the sun rising over the city below. "But I figured it's now or never."

"Why Barbados?"

"My family has a little beach house there. I haven't been there in years, but it's private enough for the two of us." Complete with an iron fence and an infinity pool with a fabulous view of the water. "Thank you for coming with me."

"Of course." He paused, his head tilted to the side. "So what happened at work? You said you turned in your story, but I know you were having a hard time writing it."

The sick feeling in her stomach now had nothing to do with the flight. "I came up with something different. It's not what she wanted, which means I'll probably come home to a termination email, but at least my conscience is at ease."

"You never told me what she wanted you to write."

"It doesn't matter anymore." She squeezed his hand

and smiled at him. She hadn't caved to the pressure because he mattered more to her than her job. "I did what I felt was right, and now I'm looking forward to a few days in the sun with you."

"Same here." He settled back in his seat and closed his eyes.

Becca chewed her bottom lip and checked the time on her phone. Five hours until they landed. Just enough time to turn her stomach into knots.

Because even though she hadn't turned in an exposé on Ethan, her story could place her back in the center of controversy once again if it was published.

Chapter Sixteen

Ethan dove into the infinity pool and swam the length of it, stopping at the wall that overlooked the Caribbean. The sun was setting over the water like a fiery red ball that blazed bright before surrendering to the night's long shadows.

Another perfect day in paradise.

"How's the water?" Becca asked behind him.

"Warm." He turned around, and his jaw dropped.

Becca stood by the pool wearing absolutely nothing. She dropped the towel in her hand and descended into the water with a sexy sway in her hips. Her eyes locked with his, seductively intense. By the time she reached him, he was fully hard and aching to be inside her.

"Are you trying to tell me something?" he asked, his voice raw with want.

She wrapped her arms around his neck and her legs around his waist, her body fitting against his like she was specifically made for just him. "It's nice having a private beach house like this, isn't it?"

"Indeed." He lowered his lips to hers in a kiss that only increased his desire. The weekend had the ideal mix of fun and sex, from the outdoor activities like sailing and snorkeling to the long, languid lovemaking sessions in the bedroom. No TV. No Internet. No interruptions. And based on the way she was responding to his touch, she craved more.

He turned her around so her back was pressed against the wall of the pool. The sunset ignited the red highlights in her hair to form a glowing crown around her head. The subtle taste of mangos lingered on her lips from earlier. Her wet skin slipped and slid against his, every movement teasing and tempting him. The sweet scent of the tropical flowers filled the air around them, mingling with the coconut shampoo she'd used earlier that day. Everything culminated in the embodiment of something from a fantasy.

And yet it was all real. This sexy, intelligent, generous woman was in his arms, making him the luckiest son of a bitch in the world.

His swim trunks started to fall, and he kicked them off. He grabbed her ass, hoisting her out of the water and to the well-cushioned outdoor sofa beside the pool. "Should I go inside and grab a condom?"

"If you want, but I did remember to take my pill today."

He hesitated, the tip of his cock hovering over the opening to her sex. "Are you saying you trust me?"

She nodded. "Do you trust me?"

He'd witnessed her take her morning pill like clockwork enough to know she wasn't trying to trap him with a pregnancy. And even if the pill failed, he wouldn't mind. He wanted a future with her. One that might even include kids someday.

But right now, he couldn't think past how wonderful she felt as he eased into her. The tight, slick heat. The way her inner walls clenched around him. The way her lips parted in a gasp when he first entered and then released a moan as he began to move inside her.

He took his time, drawing out each exquisite stroke. This may be a one-time deal or it might be the first of many, but he was determined to savor every moment of this experience. Her body rose to meet his like the waves on the shore. He laced his fingers through hers while his mouth devoured hers in one passionate kiss after another. And when he took her over the edge, he held her tightly as he followed.

When the world came back into focus, night had fallen. Solar lights illuminated the paths through the garden leading back to the house, and the quarter moon overhead provided just enough light for him to see her face. Her beauty nearly took his breath away, but the glow in her eyes made his heart skip a beat.

She gave him a shy smile as she reached up to stroke his face, trailing her fingers along his jaw. "I love you," she whispered.

Time seemed to freeze, but instead of being terrified, he welcomed it. This was a moment he wanted to last forever, to commit to his memory. Once he'd memorized every detail, he brushed a lock of hair back from her forehead and said, "I love you, too, Becca."

Her smile widened, and she pulled him down to another kiss.

And he couldn't think that his life could be more

perfect than right now.

***

Ethan's phone rang, pulling him from the last blissful remnants of sleep. He saw Adam's name on the screen and hurried out of the bedroom before the call woke Becca.

"Hi, Adam," he answered while throwing on a bathrobe. "How are you this morning?"

"A little annoyed. Why didn't you tell me you were dating Becca Shore?"

It looked like it was shaping up to be another gorgeous day in paradise, but the coldness in Adam's voice carried over the phone and raised gooseflesh on Ethan's arms. "Because I knew you'd have a shit fit like this."

He could hear his older brother seething on the other end as he struggled to get his anger in check. "So you knew she'd be trouble."

"Trouble? No way." He hopped up on the counter and reached for a glass of water. "If anything, she's been the best thing that's ever happened to me."

"Then you haven't seen the news yet."

His mouth went dry. "What are you talking about?"

"Turn on the TV."

"I can't."

"Why not?"

"Because there isn't one in this house." His heart started pounding, and his mind leapt in a hundred different directions, none of them good. "Tell me what's going on, Adam."

"She sold you out."

The glass started to slip from his hand, and he set it

down before he dropped it and the crash woke her up. "What are you talking about?"

"Just that. Apparently, she sold an exclusive story to some women's magazine called *Moderne* about you, and the media's been buzzing about it. The issue will be out tomorrow, but the editor, Elaine Halpern, leaked some photos of the two of you looking rather cozy together while ice skating."

"Fuck!" Ethan jumped off the counter and paced the room, raking his fingers through his hair. "How did she get those?"

"From your girlfriend, obviously. She probably set you up."

"Becca's not like that." And yet that little niggle of doubt refused to disappear. Too many things didn't add up. Her secrecy about the story she had to turn in. The sudden funds to fly them first class to Barbados. The beach house that was completely cut off from all media.

"Okay, let's forget her father still probably bears a grudge against us for the Michigan Avenue property—which I should've picked up on when you were asking about him. Let's forget she doesn't have the most stellar reputation, either, and is probably jumping at the chance to make headlines again. Can you imagine how much she's getting paid to dish out the dirt on you?"

"And I'm telling you, Becca's not like that."

"Really? You don't sound so convinced." The clicking sounds on a keyboard followed. "It says here that the story will reveal details about your addiction, your recovery, and your upcoming solo project. If she didn't provide those details, who did?"

His head swam, and he sank down onto the sofa before his knees refused to hold him up any longer. There was no other explanation. Becca had betrayed him. The fucking bitch had lured him there, told him she loved him, and made him admit he loved her, too, all while trying to keep him from learning the truth.

"Where are you now?" Adam asked, his voice devoid of the anger from earlier.

"Barbados."

"Want me to book you on the next flight out?"

His gut recoiled at the pity in his brother's voice, at the idea of Adam having to bail him out once again, but part of him was glad to have someone looking out for him. "Please."

A few more clicks on a keyboard followed. "There's one leaving in two and a half hours."

"I can make it." He'd take the Jeep they'd rented, even if it meant leaving her stranded. After all, she'd probably made enough money from selling him out to afford a taxi back to the airport.

"Got you booked."

"Thanks, Adam." He hung up, his hands shaking. For the first time in months, he was more than tempted to shoot up and just forget about the world, but he refused to relapse because of a two-timing woman. He knew he needed to confront her, to tell her it was over, but the center of his chest ached over the prospect of doing it.

He still loved her.

Which made her betrayal that much harder to bear.

But I have to do this.

He banged the bedroom door open, his hands clenched

into determined fists.

Becca jumped up, her eyes wide with fear. "Ethan, what's wrong?"

"I know what you did." He tried to sound hard and furious, yet the moment his eyes raked down her naked curves, he found his resolve crumbling.

Damn it, I still want her.

He grabbed his bag and started stuffing his things into it to keep from touching her and losing all self-control.

"What are you talking about?"

"Congratulations, Becca. You finally had your big break. Your story about me is all over the news."

"What the hell are you talking about?" She gathered the sheet around her and moved toward him, but he snatched his bag out of her way and went into the bathroom to grab the rest of his things.

"No wonder you were all closed off about that story your editor wanted you to turn in. You were figuring out the best way to betray me." He came back in and pulled on a pair of jeans. "And I'm sure you probably paid that photographer at Wollman Rink to take photos of us, too, just to seal the deal."

"Ethan, no." Her mouth hung open in disbelief. "I didn't do any of that."

"But you knew, didn't you? How else did your editor get those photos?"

She crossed her arms around her stomach and looked as though she was about to puke. A confession of guilt if he'd ever saw one.

"All this talk about protecting me, about respecting my privacy." He yanked on a T-shirt and grabbed the keys on the nightstand. "It was all a pack of lies to gain my trust so you could sell me out the moment you had the highest bidder."

Tears filled her blue-green eyes, and her chin trembled. "You really think that of me?"

He paused, and for a split second, he wondered if he'd jumped to the wrong conclusion. "What else am I to think when the magazine you work at is coming out tomorrow with an exclusive story all about me?"

She squeezed her eyes shut, releasing one lone tear in the process. But she clenched her teeth, and when she opened her eyes again, they were hard and cold. "This whole time, after I've gone out of my way to keep your identity a secret, you think I would stage photos and blab all your secrets to Elaine? What happened to you trusting me to do the right thing?"

"Obviously, I was wrong about you."

She shook, but more from rage than sadness this time. Her finger pointed toward the door. "Get out!"

"Gladly." He turned around and left before his gut checked him and made him look back. Maybe once he got home, he could sulk over his broken heart and beat himself up for being such an idiot.

But right now, he had a plane to catch.

***

Becca waited for the rumbling of the Jeep's engine to fade before she let the sob choking her throat escape. No matter what she did, it was doomed to blow up in her face.

She'd turned in an article exposing her own story of addiction and recovery, and yet Elaine had chosen to weave her version about Ethan, no doubt fed by info from

Daddy and Claire. And what was worse, Ethan had chosen to believe she'd sold him out.

The sobs intensified, and she buried her face in the pillow to muffle them. When she reached the point where she couldn't cry any more, she crawled out of bed and into the shower. The hot water washed away the salt of her tears and eased the pain of her breaking heart.

Her flight didn't leave until Wednesday morning. That gave her two days to come up with a plan to exact revenge against Elaine and her parents. But there was no hope getting Ethan back. As much as she loved him, he didn't trust her when it mattered the most. And without trust, they had no future together.

Chapter Seventeen

Becca came out of the terminal at JFK with her hat pulled low and her eyes downcast. She'd gotten a glimpse of the cover of the latest issue of *Moderne* on the airport's newsstands, and she didn't want anyone to recognize her as she made her way to baggage claim to grab her suitcase.

A sharp whistle made her stop short and look up.

Jacob stood in line with the drivers holding cards with people's names on them. He wore a silly grin on his face and held his own sign that said "Big Sis" in bright blue sloppy letters.

She made her way over to him. "What are you doing here?"

"What does it look like I'm doing? I'm here to give you a ride home." He leaned over and whispered, "By the way, if you want to keep your travel plans a secret, don't use Dad's credit card. The minute he saw the charge, he knew what flight you'd be on and sent me to fetch you."

"So I'm being kidnapped and brought before him to answer for my actions?"

"Ouch! Lighten up, Becca. It's the first night of Hanukkah, after all." He took her carry-on bag and moved them toward baggage claim. "Although I do kind of like the idea of being a bounty hunter."

"I have nothing to say to him, you know."

"Maybe it will be different this time." He grabbed her suitcase from the carousel. "By the way, where's Ethan?"

"He broke up with me and flew home two days ago. Accused me of blabbing all his secrets to the highest bidder."

Jacob winced. "That sucks. I actually liked him."

"Me, too. But you know how Daddy can be when he doesn't get his way."

"Are you suggesting he did something to break you two up?" Jacob led her outside to where he'd parked his Mini Cooper.

"Of course I am. After all, he and Claire were the ones who told Elaine we were dating." She climbed into the passenger seat and waited while her brother threw her bags into the back.

Jacob got behind the wheel, but didn't start the engine right away. "Listen, Becca, I don't know all the details, but Dad sent me to pick you up because he wanted to talk to you about something, and I think you should at least hear him out before you tell him to fuck off again."

"I doubt he has anything to say that will make amends for what he's done, but whatever."

As Jacob drove back into the city, Becca asked how things were going at Yale, how his classes were going, if he was dating anyone. The distraction soothed her sullen mood until they got to her parents' house. She climbed out the car, dreading every step that brought her closer to confronting her father for the second time in less than a week.

The smell of frying latkes greeted her when she opened the front door. Claire appeared from the living room with her arms outstretched, pulling her into a hug. "Happy Hanukkah, Becca."

She stayed stiff and aloof, not returning her stepmother's affection. After all, she was a member of the party who'd fed information to Elaine. "Hi, Claire."

Claire stepped back, a frown creating the slightest of wrinkles in her otherwise flawless Botoxed face. She looked to Jacob for an explanation, but he simply shrugged. The awkward tension continued to grow until she clasped her hands together and said politely, "Your father wishes to speak to you in his study."

"Let's get this over with so I can get home and start prepping my résumé." She didn't even bother taking her coat off before making her way to the room in the back of the house with the imposing polished walnut shelves housing rare first editions of classic works of literature mixed in with photographs of some of Shore Hotels' more extravagant resorts. This would be a short visit.

The door was open, and her father sat behind his desk, reading something on his computer. He didn't even look up until she cleared her throat. "Rebecca, close the door and have a seat."

"No, Daddy, let's keep this short, shall we? Congratulations. You not only managed to cost me my job—which you got me in the first place—but you also cost me a relationship with a great guy. So I hope you're happy."

She turned to leave, but the stern tone of her father's

voice stopped her. "I said close the door and have a seat."

She shut the door and plopped down in the leather armchair he was pointing to, unbuttoning her coat in the process. "Whatever you have to say—"

"I will say it, and you will keep your mouth shut until I'm finished." He came around his desk and sat down in the matching armchair on the other side of the small round end table. "I had another interesting luncheon with Elaine on Friday."

"Where you probably told her everything else you could about Ethan so she could publish her exposé."

"I said, let me finish." He crossed his arms and squinted one eye as he studied her. "She said she'd given you that assignment, and you'd refused to do it. Why?"

"Because he was my boyfriend. We'd both worked so hard to keep our relationship out of the media spotlight. And more important, it was wrong. It was a violation of trust. But thanks to you and Elaine, he thinks I did it anyway."

"I never thought she'd take what I told her over lunch to such extremes." Her father looked down and away, sliding one hand down his cheek to his chin. "So I assume that the feature in *Moderne* caused some tension between you two."

"He dumped me in Barbados, just like you wanted."

"I never said I wanted that." His voice stayed calm and steady, but anger flashed in his eyes.

"No, you didn't, but based on the way you treated him at Thanksgiving, you don't like him either. I bet you'll do a little happy dance after I leave."

"Rebecca." He said her name as a warning and shifted

in his chair. "Elaine, however, did forward me a copy of the article you turned in."

She braced for the lecture on how her story of addiction and recovery would be a smear on the Shore family name, but her father remained quiet and pensive as though he was choosing his next words carefully.

"It was a very powerful piece."

All the air fled her lungs. He was actually giving her praise. "Did I hear you correctly?"

He gave her one slow nod. "It got me thinking about what you said in my office last week about wanting to bring about change and raise awareness. At first, I thought you were suffering from some kind of delusion, but once I read that story...."

His mouth started twitching, and he pressed his finger against his lips to still them. "You are actually a very gifted writer, Rebecca."

Her head swam. That was the second time he'd said something positive about her in the last five minutes. Any more praise, and the world might start spinning in the opposite direction. "Um, thank you."

"It made me realize how far you've come and that maybe I should give you another chance. Furthermore, once I read that article, I told Elaine your talents were being wasted at a trashy magazine like hers and were better suited for more serious publications."

She bit her bottom lip to keep from laughing at the shocked expression Elaine must have worn when he said that.

"And the funny thing is, she agreed with me." Her father leaned forward, scooting his chair toward her. "She mentioned some of the topics you'd brought up at the staff meetings. It seems you have quite the drive for social justice and awareness."

"I want to be something more than just some spoiled little rich girl."

"And I'm beginning to see that you are." He sat back on the chair and drummed his fingers on the armrests. "It seems you aren't the only member of the family who wanted to make the world a better place. Before your grandfather died, he set up the Shore Foundation as a charitable trust. I've been too busy running the business to pay much attention to it, and I'm afraid the foundation has fallen to the wayside. Perhaps it's time I placed someone in charge of it who could put it to good use."

He paused and stared directly at her.

Her heart fluttered as the implications of his offer sank in. "You want me to take over the foundation?"

He gave another single, slow nod. "You seem to have the drive for it, and if you can continue to write passionate, persuasive articles like the one you turned into Elaine, I have a feeling you might just make the world a better place."

"And you don't think I'll screw it up or pilfer funds to buy drugs?"

This time, he shook his head. "No, I think you've shown you can be trusted."

Her hands trembled, and her voice shook as she said, "I don't know what to say."

"Understandable. Of course, I haven't disclosed the complete terms of this position. You will receive a small stipend for compensation, as well as any necessary travel expenses to set up projects you deem important. It will come with the standard Shore Hotels corporate benefits, and—"

She silenced him by throwing her arms around him in a hug. "I accept the job, Daddy."

He balked at first, then very slowly wrapped his arms around her and returned the hug. "I'm very proud of you."

Her throat choked up, and despite her best efforts to stop them, a few renegade tears slipped out. Her whole life, she'd felt like she'd always be a disappointment to her father. She never dreamed she'd hear him say he was proud of her. She pulled back and wiped her cheeks with the back of her hand. "I bet you've never had an employee break down in tears over being offered a job."

"True, but then, I've never hired my daughter before, either. I know I've been hard on you in the past, but I truly believe the foundation will be in good hands now." He patted her on the arm and gave her an apologetic smile. "Why don't we join Claire and Jacob for some latkes?"

"Sounds fabulous." She slipped off her coat and hung it up by the door before joining her family in the dining room.

The sun had set well over an hour ago, but the two candles in the Hanukkah menorah still cheerfully burned in the window overlooking Central Park. As soon as she sat down at the table, Mrs. Cordero appeared from the kitchen and set a plate of steaming hot latkes in front of her. Jacob passed her the sour cream and applesauce, and she shared her good news with the rest of the family.

But despite the excitement of celebrating the holiday

with her family, part of her still mourned the end of her relationship with Ethan. Claire seemed to pick up on it first and asked about him.

"He didn't believe me when I told him I hadn't leaked the details of his personal life to Elaine," Becca replied with a shrug, even though his accusations still stung. "If he doesn't trust me, then what hope do we have for a solid relationship?"

Her father and Claire held hands and looked at each other before her stepmother said, "We're the ones who told Elaine about him, and if there's anything we can do to help make amends—"

"Don't bother." The flavorful latkes turned to dry mush in her mouth, and she pushed her plate away. "What's done is done."

"Then I guess your feelings for him must have been lukewarm at best," her father replied, "if you're not willing to fight to get him back."

She curled her fingers into her palms, her heart still aching for him. "What do you suggest I do, Daddy? He didn't believe me. He thought the worst of me when it mattered the most, and...." She drew in a deep breath to regain her composure. "I won't grovel and ask for forgiveness when I did nothing wrong."

"Then maybe you should give your side of the story."

"I'm not going to the news station and airing my dirty laundry for the entire world, Daddy. I've caused enough scandal as it is."

"Understandable. The question is," her father continued, "do you want us to interfere in your personal life?"

She chewed her bottom lip and considered his offer. The last three years, she'd done everything she could to break off ties to her family and be independent, but this might be the one time when she gracefully accepted their assistance. "What's your plan?"

Her father gave her a shrewd smile. "Wait and see. In the meantime, you need your own platform for the stories you want to tell." Her father turned to Jacob. "Maybe you can help your sister create one of those blog things to get her message across for the Shore Foundation."

"I'd love to," her brother said with a grin.

Chapter Eighteen

Ethan shivered at the end of Pier 84 and stared into the choppy waters of the Hudson. A storm was rolling in, and the usually busy park was deserted. During the ten minutes he'd been there, he hadn't stumbled across a single soul. The last time he'd come here, Becca had saved him from falling back to his former muse. But since he'd left her in Barbados a week ago, he'd felt more lost than ever. The music had dried up, and his dreams at night were haunted by the hurt on her face when he'd walked out on her. And he didn't want to think about the desire to fall back on his old addictions.

He'd picked up an issue of the magazine and found the details on the story it contained to be superficial at best. Definitely not the tell-all it promised to be, which made him wonder if Becca wasn't the leak after all. There were enough photos of them together, but they all dated back to Thanksgiving. Nothing before then.

Then he'd heard the news that she'd been appointed to head up the Shore Foundation and read the first two articles she'd posted on the foundation's blog. The first one was about reshaping the foundation's direction, and the second one was a gritty, unapologetic piece about addiction and how it defied stereotypes. In footnotes, she mentioned that the article had originally been submitted to *Moderne* magazine, but it was rejected because it was deemed unsuitable for the magazine's readership.

But it spoke to him and filled in the missing pieces of the puzzle. It was the article she'd turned in to take the place of the tell-all her editor wanted.

He pulled out his phone and found her number. Seconds ticked by as he stared at it, but he couldn't bring himself to call her. His stomach churned like the river in front of him, and a different sort of craving filled him—one for her.

He called Adam instead. "Talk me off a ledge."

"Why?" Worry laced his older brother's voice. "Are you thinking of using again?"

"No. I'm thinking about calling her."

"Becca Shore?"

"No, Marilyn Monroe. Of course I'm talking about Becca."

"Why?"

He shuffled his feet and kicked the railing. "I miss her."

"Even after the article?"

"Yeah." He paused and added, "The funny thing is, I don't think she was the one who sold me out. I mean, the things in that article could've come from anyone at the Thanksgiving table. She has a lot more dirt on me than that."

"So what are you saying?"

"I think I made a huge mistake."

He waited for Adam to tear into him like he did last

week, but instead, his brother said, "I had a nice long conversation with her father today about a business proposition, and when the conversation turned to her, some very interesting information turned up and made me realize that maybe I misjudged her, too."

"Whoa! Did I just hear you admit that you were wrong? Mr. 'I Know It All and Never Make A Bad Decision'?"

Adam chuckled. "Yeah, being married has taught me some humility."

"Any chance you could pass some of those lessons on to me?"

"Are you saying you want her back?"

"More than anything. She steadies me. She inspires me. She keeps me going when I feel like I can't. She's my muse, and without her, I feel like there's a part of me missing." Ethan held his breath and rubbed at the hollow feeling that lingered in the center of his chest. "I still love her."

"Then maybe you should turn around and tell me that," a woman said behind him.

He turned around to find Becca standing a few feet away. "I'll call you back later," he murmured before hanging up on Adam. "What are you doing here?"

"Looking for you." She stayed where she was, her hands in the pockets of her jacket. The wind whipped her dark hair around her face. "I was just outside your place, actually, when you rode off. Thankfully, the cab driver was willing to follow you."

Hope flared within him. Maybe she'd been missing him as much as he missed her. "Why were you coming to my place?"

She looked down at the ground. "It's Monday, and I was just coming over to make sure you'd be at the NA meeting tonight. I'm still here for you, Ethan. At least, until you decide on an official sponsor."

"How long were you standing there?"

"Long enough." He expected her to close the gap between them, but she remained as still as a statue.

The message was loud and clear. She wanted him to take the first step.

His tongue felt twice its normal size as he stumbled over the words he knew she needed to hear. "I'm sorry, Becca. I shouldn't have accused you of selling me out."

"But you did."

"And I was an idiot to think that of you." He took that first step, waiting to see if she'd bolt before taking another. "I should've listened to my heart. I should've believed in you."

Her face remained unreadable as he closed the gap between them and cupped her icy, windblown cheeks in his hands, lifted her chin up so he could see into her blue-green eyes. They glittered with tears, and her bottom lip trembled, but still, she said nothing.

"Please, give me another chance, Bec."

"If we don't have trust…"

"I do trust you." He covered her lips with his own in a pleading kiss that begged her to believe him. "You know my heart, my soul, better than anyone else, and there's no one I would rather share my secrets with." His voice broke as he added, "Without you, I'm lost."

She pressed her forehead against his and released a heavy sigh. "Say it, Ethan. I need to hear you say it."

A Seductive Melody

"I love you, Becca." He placed a kiss on her forehead and wrapped his arms around her. "You get me."

She tucked her head under his chin and held on to him. "I love you, too."

And in that moment, he'd found the one thing that filled the void inside him.

Chapter Nineteen

Nothing had prepared Becca for Christmas Eve with the Kelly family. Ethan had warned her that he had six brothers, but when they arrived at his mother's home in Chicago, she was ambushed by a massive white dog that knocked her into one of the snow drifts lining the driveway and started licking her face.

"That means he likes you," a silver-haired woman shouted from the front door.

"No, Jasper's just a menace." Ethan shooed the dog away and helped her up, brushing the snow off her before leading her up the stairs. "Mom, this is Becca."

His mother threw her arms around her in a hug. "So glad to finally meet you."

The last of the jitters faded away. After all the hoopla last week, she'd expected his family to give her the cold shoulder, but as Ethan introduced her to each of his brothers, they all greeted her with the same warmth as their mother.

The crowded house was filled with boisterous conversations as each brother tried to talk over the others. The smells of fir trees and gingerbread permeated the rooms, so different from the scent of fried foods she was accustomed to at this time of the year. Before she knew what was happening, she'd been recruited to help out in the kitchen. Adam's wife, Lia, assigned her to add the finishing touches to the mashed potatoes that would go with the massive prime rib she was carving.

By the time dinner was done, she'd felt like she was already part of the family. Ben and his wife teased for her being a Rangers fan while Frank heckled her for rooting for the Giants. She found out that Gideon's next project would be a movie with Ari's brother, and she warned him about Gabe's habit of playing practical jokes on the set. She admired photos of the car Caleb and his wife, Alex, were restoring and sighed over the way Dan fawned over his pregnant girlfriend, Jenny.

The family retreated to the living room after dinner, but Ethan pulled her aside and pointed to the branch of mistletoe hanging above them.

"I don't think that's a Hanukkah tradition," she teased.

"Humor me." He tilted her face up and kissed her until she was breathless.

"Get a room, you two," Frank teased, bumping into Ethan as he passed them.

Ethan gave the massive linebacker a playful shove, which evolved into playful roughhousing until their mother broke it up with a sharp "Boys!"

Mrs. Kelly then looped her arm through Becca's, saying, "They never grow up."

"We've got to keep you on your toes, Mom," Ethan said, placing a kiss on his mother's cheek before stealing Becca back. "We'll join you in a moment."

He led her back into the dining room and pulled out the distinctive little blue and white box that could only come from Tiffany's. "I know Hanukkah ended today, but better late than never, right?"

Her pulse quickened as she untied the ribbon. The box was the perfect size for a ring, even though her mind told her it was still too early for that. After all, they'd just admitted they loved each other a little over a week ago.

She opened the lid to find a diamond and platinum key pendant instead and released the breath she'd been holding.

"Expecting something different?" he asked, his gray eyes filled with mirth.

"More like relieved." She pulled the necklace out and admired the way it sparkled. "It's gorgeous."

"Just like you." He took the necklace and fastened it around her neck. "I'm trusting you with the key to my heart."

"And I promise not to break it."

"I know." He pressed lips to hers before whispering in her ear, "But if it had been a ring?"

"I might've said yes," she teased. "After all, you get me."

He laughed before giving her a passionate kiss that made her heart sing and promised her a future of many more in the days to come.

A Note to Readers

Dear Reader,

Thank you so much for reading *A Seductive Melody*. I hope you enjoyed it and look forward to the next book in the series, *In the Red Zone*. If you did, please leave a review at the store where you bought this book or on Goodreads.

I love to hear from readers. You can find me on Facebook and Twitter, or you can email me using the contact form on my website, www.CristaMcHugh.com.

If you would like to be the first to know about new releases or be entered into exclusive contests, please sign up for my newsletter using the contact form on my website at http://bit.ly/19EJAW8.

Also, please like my Facebook page for more excerpts and teasers from upcoming books. And, just for this series, I have a special website featuring more information on the Kelly Brothers, playlists, recipes, and other extras just for readers. Please check it out at www.thekellybrothers.cristamchugh.com.

--Crista

Don't miss the next book in the Kelly Brothers series…

In the Red Zone

The Kelly Brothers, Book 6

When scandal rocks their relationship, will their chances for a happy ending be fourth and long?

Coming in February 2015…

Sign up for Crista's Newsletter to be the first to know when *In the Red Zone* is available.

Author Bio

Growing up in small town Alabama, Crista relied on storytelling as a natural way for her to pass the time and keep her two younger sisters entertained.

She currently lives in the Audi-filled suburbs of Seattle with her husband and two children, maintaining her alter ego of mild-mannered physician by day while she continues to pursue writing on nights and weekends.

Just for laughs, here are some of the jobs she's had in the past to pay the bills: barista, bartender, sommelier, stagehand, actress, morgue attendant, and autopsy assistant.

And she's also a recovering LARPer. (She blames it on her crazy college days)

For the latest updates, deleted scenes, and answers to any burning questions you have, please check out her webpage, www.CristaMcHugh.com.

Sign up for Crista's 99c New Release Newsletter at http://bit.ly/19EJAW8

Find Crista online at:

Twitter: twitter.com/crista_mchugh

Facebook: www.facebook.com/CristaMcHugh

CPSIA information can be obtained at www.ICGtesting.com
Printed in the USA
LVOW07s0844161114

413957LV00007B/950/P